Cynder
in the
Garden of Lapis

C. Logan Anthony, PhD

i

DEDICATION

I want to thank my husband, Steve, for his faith in me and his continued guidance. Thanks to my two daughters; Carmen and Audra, for sticking by me in my quest to write, to my granddaughter, Johnna, for reading and critiquing chapters at the early stages of this book, to my grandson, Reid, for reading my magazine articles and respecting me as a writer. Special thanks to my niece, Nicole Loughan, for her advice and guidance as an established writer. Thanks also to my longtime friend, Kristie, and her son for influencing and encouraging this story. Special thanks to my friend, Ellen, for her loyal support and hard work in helping proof the novel, and to Barbara for her emotional support and other members of my writing group for encouraging me to get my first novel published. Also many thanks to my sister-in-law, Patty, for her assistance.

Cover illustration, design, and production by
Center for Success, LLC Publishing Company

acenterforsuccess.com

Happiness depends upon ourselves. –Aristotle

∞

CYNDER

IN

THE

GARDEN

OF

LAPIS

CONTENTS

CHAPTER ONE

When curiosity drove fourteen-year-old Cynder Zappa to enter her mother's private world of magic, she prepared for the worst. Her mother would be in town only a little while. This would give Cynder a short time alone in the house.

She took a deep breath and stepped into her mother's bedroom. She ran her dirty hands down her dingy-white dress and knelt beside the bed, searching for the old wooden box. She spotted it between dust bunnies, tucked her stringy hair behind her ears, and reached out to the handle on the side, afraid for her life. She carefully tugged the box from under the bed as though it held a live bomb.

Normally Cynder wouldn't go through her mother's things, especially her magic things; she had never really been interested in magic. She thought Mother's magic was silly and immature. She dreaded when she brought out the old wooden box, her magic box, she called it.

The box was two-and-a-half-feet-long and one-foot-wide. It was the box her mother had used for her private possessions ever since she was a little girl. In large block letters the words "Jessilyn's Magic Box" were written on the top in black paint. A large and unusually shaped star was carved in the top and traced with yellow paint.

Cynder ran her hands over the box. She was about to enter into a secret world that her mother always held sacred. She dragged it down the hallway into her room, shut and locked the door, pulled the blinds, and flipped the light on. A part of her was afraid of what she would find and the other part of her was curious. Her stomach was in knots and her hands were as slippery as a frog. She would never be the same after this.

The last thing she wanted to do was venture into this box, but earlier that morning unforeseen events brought Cynder to communicate with a nature spirit in her sacred garden. She was told there were clues in the box that would answer her questions.

That morning started off as any other day would in her house on the first Saturday of summer break. Cynder fought with her mother and then fled the house to be alone in her garden where few ventured to go.

Cynder saw her mother's best friend and her son, Sheridan, pull into the driveway. As usual Sheridan came to the garden to talk to Cynder.

"They're doing it again," Cynder said. She dropped

effortlessly from high up in the tree. She adjusted her dress and pulled her blue stone necklace into place. "Our Moms and their magic stuff… abracadabra," she said, and rolled her eyes and made fun of them by waving her hands around.

"Aw Cynder, let them have their fun, they aren't hurting anybody." Sheridan said. "They've been doing that stuff for a long time and it's their girl time together."

Cynder's mother, Jessilyn and Sheridan's mother had been best friends since college. Cynder called Sheridan's mother Aunt Krystal.

Sheridan looked up in the tree from where she'd just dropped down; "Don't you ever get tired of climbing trees? Sometimes I think you live in them."

"No I don't get tired of climbing and sometimes I do wish I lived in them…alone." She tugged fiercely at the hose on the ground and struggled to pull it across the garden. "And my name is Cynthia; remember, I asked you to call me that now."

Cynder's mother had been calling her Cynder since she was little. Ever since Cynder turned fourteen she felt she was too old for a nickname, but not for climbing trees.

"I can't have friends over when they perform their magic stuff, it's embarrassing," Cynder said, pulling the hose around to water a bed of flowers in the corner of the garden.

"I'm your only friend and I come over all the time," Sheridan said, "especially when they're doing their magic." He pretended to stumble and mock her magic arms maneuvers.

Cynder turned the hose on him. He laughed and put his hand up. "Okay enough."

She knelt down to a bed of flowers gently petting them as though they were cherished pets. She whispered to them, but he ignored her. He learned a long time ago that what she whispered to them was private between Cynder and her flowers. Sometimes he felt like she did that just to bug him.

Sheridan was the only kid she talked to. She never felt comfortable with those her own age. Cynder was quiet and somber most of the time, and preferred to be alone. Sheridan was three years older than Cynder; he was tall and athletic, and made friends easily.

Sheridan sat down on the cement bench and picked up an urn that sat beside him. He wondered why he had never noticed the decorated pottery piece before now. He swiveled it around, looking at the painted fairies that decorated it.

"What is this thing?"

"It's my grandma's ashes," Cynder said.

The thought of holding someone's ashes caused Sheridan to bolt upright. The urn slipped from his lap. He lifted his leg straight out and stopped it with his foot before it hit the ground. Once he got it secured on his lap again, he held it more carefully. "That's not funny Cynder," he said.

"I'm not joking, those are her ashes. I found it up in the attic. Mother must have put it up there to hide her from me."

"How do you know it's her?"

"Because her name, birth date, and date of her death are etched on the bottom of the urn."

Sheridan carefully held it up and read the bottom of it. Cynder was right; her grandmother's information was etched on the bottom along with the creator's information. "Designed by JT?" Sheridan said. "What kind of a weirdo would design something like this for a person's ashes?"

"I don't know… I think it's kinda cool. Maybe that's why your mom gave me all those fairy statues, because I didn't know my grandma. Maybe my grandma liked fairies."

Sheridan shrugged his shoulders and sat it back on the bench.

As Jessilyn and Krystal settled into their seats at the kitchen table, Jessilyn said, "I wish Cynder wasn't so unhappy. I wish she'd find another interest besides that garden." She opened the magic box and pulled out a large cloth and a box of Tarot cards.

"Sheridan is going to ask her to help out at the school. He's starting on Monday," Krystal said. "This would be a great opportunity for both of them. I think she'll find helping out at the school to be fulfilling for her."

"I wish Cynder could make some friends though."

"I know," Krystal agreed, "She will be in school with Sheridan this next school year, but he has friends of his own.

I know Sheridan loves her like a little sister, but he won't want her around all of the time."

"I understand that. She needs to meet someone she can share her feelings with. She has so much that I know she isn't sharing with me. I'm afraid she never will. The last thing I want to do is have our relationship turn out the way my mom and I did." Jessilyn said a silent 'I wish' statement for Cynder in her head and asked the nature spirits for help. She handed Krystal the cards.

"What question are you seeking for answers from the Tarot today Jess?"

"Will help be sent for me and Cynder?"

Sheridan got up from the bench and stood next to Cynder. "My mom wanted me to talk to you about some volunteer work available at the new autistic school this summer. She thinks that you could make it look nice by planting some flowers around the yard and in the gardens. The place is huge and they want to make it look impressive. Mom says the owner is rich and will spend a small fortune to make it look better. He owns the old Pleiades Hotel at the edge of the city, so they're turning that into the school. I'm going to work there too. I can pick you up Monday morning."

Sheridan knew Cynder would follow him anywhere he went. Cynder was his little shadow.

"Does your mom think I know enough to pick out flowers and plant them for a place that special?"

"You know more about gardening flowers than anyone I know Cynder, and mom told them that you really know what you're doing."

Krystal had always treated Cynder special and thought the world of her. When Cynder was eight, she got her a fairy statue that looked just like her. The fairy had long, dark blonde hair, pale skin, a simple white dress, and she even wore a dark-blue stone necklace, like Cynder's. The only thing the fairy had that Cynder didn't was delicate glittery turquoise butterfly wings.

Sheridan was glad that Cynder was interested in the summer work at the autistic school. At least she would be around other people. He and his mother were hoping that she could meet some kids her own age.

Cynder had trouble making friends and never fit in with anyone her age. The girls at school called her Cinderella, and she wasn't even a step-sister. They had no idea that she spent most of her time in the garden or in a tree and that her hands were stained from gardening. And with Cynder always wearing white, it was hard for her to keep clean. Grand Aster was a small city, and there was little chance for Cynder to meet anyone new to make friends with.

Cynder walked to a bed of flowers and got on her knees. She turned the dirt with her trowel and tossed the weeds over her shoulder. Dirt from the roots showered her but she didn't seem to mind that her hair and clothes became peppered with black dirt.

Cynder ran her dirt-stained hands delicately down the flower's long stems. "These beautiful flowers, called Gaillardia, are named after the man that discovered them, M. Gaillard de Charentonneu," she said. "Sometimes he called them blanket flowers, because the bright colors reminded him of the brightly patterned blankets made by Native Americans that settled here in Michigan. Isn't that interesting? I dug some up and brought them from the beach a few years ago. I know, I'm not supposed to take them from the beach, but I wanted them. Look at how nicely they've filled out. They are from a family of sunflowers, only they're more colorful than ordinary sunflowers."

The flowers stood majestic at a foot and a half tall with the head of the flower the size of Cynder's hand. The ruby colored centers made the petals of florescent oranges, yellows, reds, and deep browns, pop out. The stems were covered with deep green leaves that kept the ground hidden beneath them. Harmless orange and brown furry caterpillars fed on them and you could find them crawling up and down the stems and leaves.

Sheridan crouched over to look more closely, because he did find the flowers interesting. He admired how much Cynder knew about the flowers in the garden and their history.

The flower drew him closer and he studied the deep colors and the patterns in the petals. Soon his face was only inches from the blooms. All of a sudden something reached out and touched his face. "Hey," he said, snapping his head back and tripping backwards. He landed on his butt with a 'thud.' He sat stunned on the ground. He shook his head from side to side. He rubbed his eyes. He rubbed his face. He rubbed his nose.

Cynder rushed over by him and stood above him. When she saw that he wasn't hurt, she let out a giggle. "What are you doing?"

He scrambled to his feet, stood back, and stared at the flowers with a frightful look on his face. "Something just reached out and touched my nose, with like --like, a hand or something."

"It was probably a caterpillar." She looked at his face; he had, what looked like, whitish-gold dust all over his face.

He shook his head, "No it was a small hand. I know it was a hand." He blinked his eyes rapidly and tried to wipe his face off with his shirt.

"A small hand from... what?" Cynder asked. Sometimes she thought she had seen things moving in the flowers too, but thought it was caterpillars or toads, or frogs from the pond at the back of the garden. "Probably just a foot from a frog or a toad."

"No Cynder, it was definitely a hand from...I don't know what it was, let's go back up to the house," Sheridan said, still rubbing his face.

"It looks like you just got too close and got pollen on yourself," she said, and eyed the bed of Gaillardia flowers.

"Well, I feel funny; it's getting late and my mom's probably ready to go, see you at eight on Monday," he said. He walked away, still dazed.

CHAPTER TWO

Cynder noticed the Gaillardia flowers looked withered and dry. She turned the hose to soaker mode. When she was watering she scanned the flowers for frogs or toads or anything that could be mistaken for the hand that Sheridan thought touched his nose.

Her mind wandered to her mother and her magic. What could she really do with it? Was she really a witch? Her face looked so sour; one would have thought she put an entire bag of Double Sour Skittles in her mouth at once. She was so deep in thought that she didn't notice that she was over-watering the plants.

"Okay, okay enough with the water now," something with a tiny voice shouted from underneath the umbrella of flowers.

Cynder couldn't believe her ears. She dropped the hose and reached down to spread the flowers apart. Sitting in a small puddle was a very wet little person, or something person-like, that was only about eight inches tall. The little person sat with one elbow propped on its knee and its chin cradled in its hand. Cynder thought it looked like a miniature girl, not much bigger than her own fairy statues. Her long, rusty-colored hair was soaked.

Droplets hung from leaves in her hair, her face, and her clothing. She had on an orange dress with stockings up to her knees and matching arm warmers that looked like fuzzy brown and orange caterpillar fur. Her bare toes and fingers were free of the stockings. She had pointy little ears and a turned up nose.

Large drops of water fell from the flowers onto her; to which she rolled her eyes and gave Cynder a dirty look.

"What are *you*?" Cynder asked. This was the first thing that popped out of her mouth. What do you say to a little person like this?

"What am I? Well I'm a fairy that is now soaked thanks to you. I noticed you like soaking people," she said, pointing to the water still running off from the leaves. "You should recognize a fairy, what with all of the fairy statues that you have."

"You know about my fairy statues?" Cynder gasped.

The fairy nodded her head and an impish grin came to her face.

"You do look like a fairy," Cynder replied, "a grouchy fairy." *Such an odd thing to say to a fairy,* she thought. But she had never talked to a fairy before.

"Well you would be grouchy too if someone was hosing you down, look at me, my wings are soaked," the fairy said. She squeezed out delicate, velvety brown and orange-striped butterfly wings, which now drooped at her sides.

"I'm sorry," Cynder said. She knelt on all fours to face her. "I...I didn't know fairies were real. Are you the one that touched my friend on the nose?"

"Yes," she giggled when she spoke, "he was right there in my face so I couldn't resist. I dusted him so he couldn't remember seeing me."

"He remembered seeing your hand," Cynder said, pointing to the fairy's hands.

The fairy nodded. "Good to know," she said, cocking her finger toward Cynder, "more fairy dust next time."

"How come you're letting me see you?"

"Cynder," she said, "your mother and Aunt Krystal have summoned the guidance of nature spirits. Since you spend most of your time in the garden, you get garden fairies."

Cynder thought that her mother and aunt were just going through the motions; she didn't realize that they could actually do anything magical.

"What are you garden fairies going to do?" Cynder was afraid. *Are they going to make me disappear?*

"We're coming to help you."

"I don't need any help," Cynder snapped. She sat upright on her knees and folded her arms in front of her.

"I was told you'd be difficult," the fairy said, rolling her eyes. She casually blew on her wings to dry them. "We will teach you to help the children."

"What children am I supposed to help? I don't know any children."

"You will know them at the school where you are going to work and you'll dream about them." The fairy said, "It's a privilege to do this work."

"I don't know if I really want to do work at that school."

"It's where you belong, Cynder."

"I really don't know where I belong." Cynder frowned.

"And you say this because?"

"I don't even know my father and my mother refuses to answer my questions. All she worries about is finding a new father for me. I don't want just any father, I want my own, my real father. She won't tell me about my grandmother or any of my family."

"I can leave you with this final thought: Your mother's magic box holds clues that will lead you to the answers you seek," the fairy announced. "The magic will happen through you…if you let it. You must look in the magic box."

"Clues? What kind of clues?" Cynder shook her head. "I don't believe in magic either, for your information."

"You are gonna be a tough one." She looked above her and a drop of water plopped in the middle of her forehead. "I gotta go someplace dryer," said the fairy. She started to leave.

"Wait, what am I supposed to call you?"

"My name is Gilly, after my flowers," she pointed at the bed of Gaillardia flowers. "Name rhymes with Lilly, the other kind of flower, not as pretty as mine, of course."

Cynder was possessive of her flowers and was a little put off by the fact that Gilly called them 'her' flowers, but she let it go for now, after all she was named after them.

Gilly pointed in the sky, took a hop, and shot into the air like a bottle rocket. Sparks trailed behind her. Then a loud 'pop' sounded in the air and she vanished. Remnants of fairy dust floated down from the air. Cynder was sure to stay away from the dust because she wanted to remember this.

Cynder slowly got up. She was so confused she didn't know what to do. She sat on the bench trying to figure out the cryptic conversation with the fairy. *What does it all mean, clues? Help the children? My mom asked for this? Magic? Mom's magic box? Is Mom really a witch?*

CYNDER

CHAPTER THREE

So now this magic box, that Cynder had always detested, became very important to her, magic or not.

Once she made sure her room was secured she pulled the box onto the braided rug next to her bed. She slowly opened up the hinged lid, not sure what she would find. It creaked when she swung the heavy top back. She half expected a rabbit or a dove to shoot forth from the box, for this was all Cynder knew of magic. She smelled aged wood, damp paper, and something sour that she could not identify.

The box was filled to the top. Cynder wasn't sure where to start. The first thing she noticed was something that she'd seen her mother pull from the box when she and Aunt Krystal practiced their magic.

Cynder carefully pulled out the rolled up cloth from under a bag of rocks, a candle, and a box of Tarot cards and spread it out on the floor. She ran her hands over it, smoothing out all the wrinkles. The cloth was the size of a large bandana and was made of canvas. It was tattered and stained. Printed at the top of the cloth were the words, 'Fairy Star.' The seven-pointed star took up most of the cloth. In the center of the star were three circles that overlapped each other. Labels on the circles said that one represented 'Body/Earth/Energy.' One said: 'Heaven/Sky/Energy,' and the other said: 'Spirit/Self/Energy.' Where they over-lapped it said 'Dreams/Energy - Fairy Land in between.'

So mother has knowledge about fairies and is working her magic through them, Cynder thought. *I thought fairies only existed in books and movies; I never thought they were real. There has to be something else in this box to answer my questions.*

After removing a few notebooks, she came to a stack of letters held together by a frayed purple ribbon. The top envelope was addressed to her mother's apartment in Texas where they had lived when Cynder was little. There was no return address. She knew it was wrong to look at any of these letters. But… without untying the bow, she carefully slid the top envelope from the stack and sat it on the cloth in the center of the star.

The envelope was bent and worn. Cynder wondered who it was from and what it said. Maybe it was a letter from the grandmother she never met.

Cynder sat and looked at it. Should she read it? She held it up to the light but couldn't see through it. She sat it back on the cloth and looked at it. She picked it up again and sniffed it, having seen this done in the movies. It just smelled old. She eased the letter out of the envelope. It was shabby as though it had been read many times. She unfolded the letter to read it.

My Dearest Jessi,

I haven't seen you for such a long time, and I miss you so much.

I wanted to let you know that I bought a small landscape and gardening nursery on the edge of Grand Aster. You know how I always loved making pottery. Well, I set up a pottery studio here to make jars for plants and flowers, but I think of these as just ordinary jars.

I make special jars for people's remains. I mean the ashes- all that are left of a person- minus their spirit. They are cremation urns. Some are large, some are small... it's the small ones that pain me most.

Some are preordered; these are the ones that are enjoyable to make. I sit down with the person and listen to their life stories while I craft the designs that best reflect their lives. No two jars are the same this way.

One old man had me put a face on his. He used marbles for eyes, then wanted his glasses put on the face once he was gone, and oh yeah... he wanted his tongue sticking out at everyone. I really liked him.

All of the art and the colors capture the child in every one of them. While we're making the jars, they tell me the story of the life they've lived and the lessons they've learned. I hear about their joys, their sorrows, and their regrets at the end of their lives. It seems to bring them peace to tell me everything.

When I present the urns to their families at the funeral I always tell of the stories as they were told to me. Their families love getting the jars at the end. They feel that they not only have the treasured ashes, but the jars and the stories as well. I rarely remember the jars, but I always remember the stories.

It's a wonderful thing when ashes are considered precious to those left behind. Ashes are not as dirty and spooky as some people portray them to be. I feel honored to be able to take a part in this process.

I love the plant business, too. It has helped me get in touch with nature, and I have learned a lot about myself. I am at peace now, but feel like something is still missing from my life.

The reason I'm writing today is because I heard, through the grapevine, that you were pregnant after our summer together and then had a daughter you named Cynder. I'm pretty sure she is mine. Why didn't you tell me? Why didn't you come back? You promised me you would be back. I waited over two years and heard nothing from you.

Don't you think it's time that Cynder met her father? I would really love to at least meet her, even if you don't want me back. I would love to help you raise 'Our Little Cynder.'

We can always work out things with your mother. Under the circumstances she should be able to put some of her feelings behind her.

I miss you and Michigan misses you too, please come back, I would love to see you and meet Cynder too!

You're in my heart always, love,

'J'

Cynder sobbed but she couldn't figure out why. Was she happy that there was a father that wanted her, or angry that her mother kept them apart?

Mother pulled up the driveway. Cynder crammed the letter back into the envelope. She jumped up to look out the window and her foot caught the letter and she kicked it under her bed.

Mother might kill her if she knew she was sneaking, so she hurried to put everything back. She put the stack of envelopes into the box and threw the bag of stones and notebooks on top of the letters. She rolled the cloth up, stuck it in the box, and put it back under her mother's bed. She ran to her bedroom, quietly closed the door, turned off her light, and pretended she was asleep.

Under the covers, Cynder rubbed the oblong stone on her necklace to comfort herself. It was half the size of her little finger and the surface was smooth. The beautiful deep-blue stone was flecked with gold and was mounted on a long silver chain. The heavy stone had served her for years as a 'worry stone,'; she rubbed it when she was nervous or upset.

Cynder's mind raced; she rubbed the stone faster and faster. *My father...my father wants to meet me?* Cynder never really felt close to her mother, she never knew how to talk to her. She had never known who her father was, and her mother never wanted to talk about him. She always picked a fight with her whenever Cynder asked about him. *He signed the letter 'J.' What does that stand for? Was it a nickname only they shared?* She now knew a little bit about him at least- he wanted to meet her. The father that never held her, never fed her a

21

bottle, and never played with her. The father that she had thought about and so badly needed. He wanted to meet her.

She wanted to read the letter again, see how long ago it had been written. She hoped that he still had a plant and pottery business on the edge of town. She would just have to find a way to locate him.

How could her mother keep this from her? Cynder wished at that moment that Jessilyn wasn't her mother, as she so often did. She wished Krystal was. Aunt Krystal never would have denied her knowing her father.

How could my mother have denied me of having a father all of this time? And if he lived here in this city, why didn't she take me to meet him?

I hate my mother.

Cynder's door creaked open; her mother entered and stood over her. Cynder held in her urge to get up and scream at her. Her mother left the room and closed her door.

Cynder cried silently as the letter that made her life more complicated than ever; lay beneath her holding keys to a long-held secret.

Sunday morning Cynder slipped out of her pajamas and into a white dress that hung on a hook on the back of her door. She rounded the corner going into the kitchen just in time to see her mother finishing her breakfast.

"Why don't you go shower and put on a clean dress?" Jessilyn urged. "You can come with me, I'm going shopping; and I'll get you some new clothes." "Just because I say you have dirty blonde hair does not mean that it should be dirty, and for heaven's sake, scrub your hands. Did you go to bed like that?"

Mother doesn't understand that true gardeners always have stains on their hands and clothes.

"I don't want to go shopping. I like my dresses and don't need any new clothes." *I wish she would just go.*

"Why can't you just try to be normal for a change?" her mother said. "Other kids might like you. You're lucky Sheridan puts up with you. You could start by dressing a little better and brushing your hair." Her mother continued to nag. "All you ever wear are those ragged white dresses. You should think about getting out of that garden and try doing something else for a change. You remind me of an old lady puttering around in that garden, just like my mother," Jessilyn said glaring at Cynder.

Cynder's white dresses were a stark contrast to the all black outfits that her mother wore. The saggy black dresses did nothing for her figure. And her long, scraggily black hair made her look scary.

"I don't want to go shopping," Cynder snapped. "I like what I wear. Why can't you just let me be me? Why do you expect me to act like other girls or dress to please anybody?"

"You're so abnormal Cynder," she said, like being different was a disease or something. "Other girls love to

23

shop." She threw her hands in the air. "Not Cynder though. No shopping for Cynder. I used to love to shop when I was your age. You are nothing like me."

Thank goodness for that, Cynder thought. "At least I don't dress like a witch."

"What do you mean by that?"

"Are you a witch mom?"

"Really, Cynder,- knock it off…now."

CYNDER

CHAPTER FOUR

Cynder woke up on Monday morning from having the strangest dream. She dreamed she was at the beach studying a bed of Gaillardia flowers up on a sand dune. She heard the sound of a little boy playing in the water on the beach about twenty feet away.

"Come play with me," he yelled in her direction.

She looked up from the flowers. *Is he talking to me?* The sun shone brightly in her eyes, but she could make out the small boy playing in the sand at the edge of the water.

"Come play with me Cinderella."

How dare that child call me Cinderella? Cynder thought in her dream state.

The sound of the waves and his voice reverberated in her head and she made her way towards him. She was ready to get after him for calling her Cinderella, she hated when people called her that.

"You will be Cinderella in the castle," he yelled, "You will save me and then I will come and save you."

He was a cute young boy of about five, with blonde wavy hair. *Innocent enough,* thought Cynder. She could tell he meant her no harm by calling her Cinderella. Still she had to correct him, because that's the kind of girl she was.

She marched up to him with one hand on her hip and the other holding a fistful of flowers with roots dangling from them. "Cinderella was not in a castle waiting to be saved," she said, "and I am not Cinderella."

"You are, you are Cinderella," he said. He gazed intently at her with eyes the most fascinating blend of green and blue that Cynder had ever seen. They looked like cracked marbles.

"You will save me and then I will save you," he repeated, smoothing the sand tower with his tiny hands.

In the dream the little boy placed a fairy statue, which looked like Cynder, at the top of the castle.

"Hey, that's my fairy statue. How did you get it?" Cynder said. She scolded him. Even in a dream Cynder was rude.

"You will save me," he repeated, "and then I will save you." He smiled as he worked diligently on the castle forming towers with buckets of sand.

Is that all he can say? Cynder thought to herself. She was becoming more and more upset with him. "Stop saying that," Cynder said through clenched teeth and she stomped her foot. "I don't even need saving."

"Yes you do," he said, "you will save me and then I will

save you." He filled another bucket with sand and flipped it making a third tower on his castle.

His words echoed in Cynder's head when she struggled to pull herself awake from her dream. She still felt angry with him when she sat up on the side of her bed, shaking her head as though she could shake the dream from her memory.

She looked at her shelf of fairies and spotted the one that looked like her. "You were the one from my dream," she whispered to the statue, "such a weird dream, next time you stay here where I left you."

CYNDER

CHAPTER FIVE

Jessilyn knocked on Cynder's door. "Cynder, Sheridan will be here soon, you need to wake up."

"Okay mom," Cynder replied, she pulled her covers over her head.

"I went shopping yesterday," her mother said, flinging Cynder's door open as she entered the room.

Cynder snapped the covers back down off her head. "Oh no, not today mom, I don't want to start out fighting about my clothes."

"It's not what you think Cynder." Her mother pulled clothes from a shopping bag. "I bought you two white dresses to wear this week. If I can't get you into anything with color, at least I can get you into one that's clean." She hung the dresses on the back of Cynder's door.

"Thanks mom," Cynder said. She forced a smile and sat up in her bed.

"Do me a favor and try not to do any gardening in these and if you have to, change your dress when you do."

"Okay mom, I will," Cynder replied. She knew she wouldn't bother to change though.

"Why are your eyes puffy? You probably slept too much. You were in bed pretty early last night."

"I need to get ready now. Can you get out?"

"Yes. I need to get ready too," her mother said. "I'll be leaving for work in a minute, have a great day."

"Sure," Cynder replied, with less excitement in her voice than her mother. "Thanks for the dresses," she murmured, and she eyed them hanging on the back of her door.

When Sheridan picked her up that morning Cynder was very quiet. She fiddled with her blue stone necklace and held it up to her face, twirling it and she watched the gold in the stone shimmer in the sunlight. She couldn't get the dream, the fairy, and her father's letter out of her head.

"Are you nervous about today?" Sheridan asked her.

When Cynder didn't react, he raised his voice and repeated his question. "I said are you nervous about today, having to work around autistic children?"

"No," she replied. She wasn't even thinking about the volunteer job yet.

"Well, you're awfully quiet."

"Yeah," she said, still concentrating on her necklace.

"What are you thinking about?"

She wasn't ready to share anything with him yet. She was still trying to sort it out in her mind. "Oh, I guess I do feel a little funny about today." She fibbed, just to keep him from probing her about what she was really thinking.

When they pulled into the parking lot Cynder was amazed by the size of the Pleiades Hotel. Back in the 1920's it had been a resort for the wealthy. Pools, fountains, and beautiful gardens had surrounded the hotel and golf course. But now everything was dilapidated from lack of care and maintenance.

The hotel was shaped like a castle, only with a modern design. Towers were placed at four corners of a section of the building. The towers had replicated turrets that were built with tiny windows only about two feet tall by a foot wide. In original castles, turrets were meant to shoot arrows and other battle weapons from and had no glass.

Cynder had seen it from the road, but never got a good look at it because the driveway to the hotel was nearly a quarter mile long. The golf course that surrounded the hotel had closed along with the hotel over 30 years ago. The Myer family owned the hotel along with the golf course and almost half of the businesses and property in Grand Aster, on the eastern shore of Lake Michigan.

Mr. Edward Aster Myer was a descendant of a business

tycoon who was the first millionaire in the United States. Mr. Myer and his wife Kalli wanted to turn the Pleiades into a school for autistics. Their adult son, Aster-Michael, was autistic and they wanted a special place for him to live that Mr. Myer could control. Their great-grandson was showing signs of being autistic also. In the past Mr. Myer didn't like the way others cared for his son in the public sector in the bigger cities. He wanted to be able to secure Aster-Michael's safety and help other autistic children in the town.

Mr. and Mrs. Myer were said to be very private people and they were getting on in age. Most of the people in the town had never seen them. They were very generous with their money though, and helped the town on many projects.

The Pleiades Hotel sign was being taken down and replaced with a grand sign that said 'School of The Pleiades.' Lighted stars graced the night blue sign with bright yellow letters. There was lots of other construction going on around the building. A team of men worked on the circular fountain at the center of the drive in front of the Pleiades. There were so many different projects going on that Cynder couldn't take it all in at once.

A small man-made river surrounded the building to give it the appearance of a moat. Many small, wooden foot bridges arched over the moat. In front of the school, two bridges were wide enough that cars and delivery trucks could cross over. Many of the bridges led to gardens or other outdoor buildings. One led to a tennis court.

"All of those little towers on that top floor go to one big room that was used as a ballroom," Cynder said.

"How do you know that?" Sheridan asked.

"I really don't know." She thought about it for a moment and didn't know how she would know that. "We get to help fix this up, that's cool."

"Yeah we do," Sheridan said. "Mom said this was going to be big, but she didn't say how big. I can't believe we're going to work here. Mom says it'll open up lots of opportunities for us and the town."

After filling out the paperwork Cynder and Sheridan got their assignments and were officially volunteers. When they got name tags Cynder was upset that hers said 'Cynder' not Cynthia. She blamed the mistake on Aunt Krystal, who gave their names to the school.

"I don't know why she doesn't realize I've grown up," Cynder told Sheridan.

He laughed at her and nudged her shoulder with his elbow. "You're fourteen and you think you're all grown up."

"I feel like I'm growing up," she told him. "I'll get Aunt Krystal to change it later."

Out of all the new employees, Cynder was by far the youngest. Many of the other employees and volunteers were parents of the autistic children, retirees, college students, teachers, and a few other high school students. Some were to work in the cafeteria, to become school janitors, to work in the housing unit, and others were assigned to the classrooms. Cynder's job was to plant flowers and other greenery on the inside and outside of the building. Sheridan was to help out wherever he was needed.

The first thing Cynder and Sheridan and a group of other new volunteers did was have a tour of The Pleiades.

"I feel like I've been here before," Cynder whispered to Sheridan.

"Not unless your mom snuck you in after it was shut down. This place hasn't been running for years."

"Well it feels like I know every room before we even walk into it. I actually have a mytical feeling inside my stomach from it."

"I think your mom is rubbing off on you," he whispered.

"She is not," Cynder growled under her breath at him and belted him in the arm with her small fist.

Sheridan laughed.

All of the new people stood before an elegantly graceful tour guide, who wanted to be called Ms. K. She was dressed in a fine suit. She wore fancy diamond rings so big that they looked too heavy for her boney hands. She had on lots of makeup and her hair was piled beautifully on top of her head. Cynder thought she looked rich and wondered why she would be working when she was extremely old.

Ms. K gave Cynder and Sheridan a look to silence them before she started the tour. She explained that the school would be fully financed for a long time to come. She said that Mr. Myer felt that adult autistics were poorly provided for, especially once their parents were gone. He wanted his son and great-grandson to be cared for by compassionate, highly trained people. He intended that the Pleiades become a center to house and educate autistic children, and even train and employ them.

"Mr. Myer," Ms. K said, "is an amateur astronomer, or star gazer, as some would call it, he gave the hotel the name of Pleiades many years ago, because Pleiades is an open seven star cluster containing hot blue, extremely luminous stars, and can be seen by the naked eye in the night sky. He thinks of the cluster as something grand and wanted a hotel to match it. Pleiades is in the constellation of Taurus and is among the nearest star clusters to Earth." She pointed at the domed ceiling in the lobby that was painted with star maps like the night sky. Bright blue ceiling lights were installed to make the stars light up. There were even stars scattered around in the tile floors. "The number seven has special significance in this cluster of stars," Ms. K said.

Cynder noticed that every time Ms. K said, 'Mr. Myer,' she pulled her shoulders back as though she were speaking of a person whom she highly respected.

Ms. K said, "Many parents feel their autistic children are 'Star Children,' 'Indigo,' or 'Crystal Children' and that they are special and highly spiritual, like angels. So, Mr. Myer feels that the stars represent the children because they shine bright too."

She went on to say that the purpose of the school was to

find special abilities in each child, whether it is art, music, or any other special talents, and help them to find ways to communicate what is inside their heads and hearts. "Mr. Myer feels that a place like this will help students to get better and to have a suitable place to learn and heal. Special food would be served to provide the best nutrition for them. In fact, the students will assist the staff in working vegetable gardens on the property."

Cynder felt connected to this place. She had never experienced feelings like this before. She could actually feel and see in her mind where flowers had been planted long ago. It was as though she were being urged by the building to replant the flowers again. She felt thrilled and scared at the same time; her heart was beating so fast, she thought it might explode. She was excited to get started in the gardens.

Throughout the rest of the school stars were the general theme. On the first story of the building, there were thirty rooms for housing, a kitchen and cafeteria, a gym, staffing offices, twelve classrooms and several large activity rooms. The second story was individual living quarters. The guide explained that they already had some students attending the private school and they would be getting more. They also had a day care program for autistic children for the summer.

Ms. K pointed out the narrow winding cement staircase that ran up the inside wall of a corner tower, just like in ancient castles. She said the staircase led to the tower ballroom on the third floor and that the room had been used in the past as a grand ballroom for large parties.

"See, told ya," Cynder whispered to Sheridan and nudged

him in the ribs.

"Mystical," he whispered back.

Cynder rolled her eyes at him.

Ms. K said that there was another set of steps in the other tower near the back of the building. This room was strictly off limits now because the windows did not meet the fire safety inspection codes that had been imposed since the hotel had been built. The windows were too narrow for escape and were not made to open. She said the room was to remain locked at all times and the keys secured in the main office.

In the afternoon Cynder and Sheridan joined Krystal in one of the classrooms.

Krystal entered the room first and announced, "This room has sand box tables, blocks, Play-Doh, and-" she stopped abruptly bringing her attention to Cynder who had come to a halt as she entered the room and was staring at a little boy who was at the sand box table.

"Are you alright Cynder?" Aunt Krystal said. She gently laid her hand on Cynder's arm. She whispered, "You'll get used to being around the autistic children."

Cynder ignored her and walked to the sand box table. It was the boy from her dream. She perched her hands on her hips, threw her shoulders back, and stepped beside him.

"What are you doing here?" she asked him. Her tone was

sharp and mean.

He didn't look at her. He continued to play, pouring sand from one bucket to the next.

Krystal got a concerned look on her face; she walked over next to Cynder. "This is Grant, he's a student," Krystal said. Her voice was gentle and understanding. "He doesn't talk."

"Yes he does," Cynder said. She moved to the other side of the sandbox table so that she could face him. "He does talk." She crouched down and looked him in the face. "Remember me? I'm Cinderella, from the beach," she said flatly.

He still didn't react to her or act like he heard her at all.

Sheridan and Krystal exchanged glances. Sheridan shrugged his shoulders and gave his mother a look of puzzlement. Krystal frowned.

"No Cynder," Krystal said. She was becoming uncomfortable. "He looks quite; um…normal, but I assure you… he doesn't speak."

"Yes," Cynder said, "he can talk Aunt Krystal." She glared at her. Cynder turned and spoke to Grant again. "Come on, save me," Cynder said shrugging her shoulders and spreading her arms out in front of her, as though she were challenging him.

An old man in the room was pulling tables around and stopped what he was doing and stared at Cynder.

Sheridan shot Cynder a look. He walked next to her and

whispered. "Cinderella?" he asked. "Save me? Stop acting weird Cynder. Why are you calling yourself Cinderella? I thought you hated that name."

Cynder then remembered that it was only a dream, an odd dream, and that it didn't really happen. But it seemed so real to her and this boy... he was the one in her dream. How and why could she have dreamed about this boy before she even met him?

"Oh it's nothing," Cynder said. She pulled herself back to reality. She assured Sheridan and Aunt Krystal she was okay. "I – I thought he was someone else."

CYNDER

CHAPTER SIX

The next four days came and went quickly. Cynder, Sheridan, and the rest of the volunteers were beginning to get used to the school and were making plans about who would work where. Cynder wasn't around Grant much, but when she was, she could get no response from him.

Cynder's mother had been home every night this week, so she couldn't get back into the magic box. She spent all her free time in her garden until nightfall and as hard as she looked Cynder saw no more fairies.

Cynder was exhausted from working hard at the school all week. Tonight her mother had a dinner meeting after work and wouldn't be home until late, so Cynder went into the magic box and retrieved the fairy cloth. She looked frantically through the box for the letter and could not locate it. *Had mother discovered that I had been into the box and removed the letter or did she take it out to reread for herself*, Cynder wondered.

Resigned to study the cloth for now, she put the box back where she found it. She took the cloth back to her room and closed and locked the door. She had no idea how to use the cloth, but she spread it out on the floor and studied it.

"Please Gilly come back," she pleaded. "And bring the other fairies too." She really didn't know the first thing about asking a fairy to come to her. She lay beside the cloth and kept her hand on it, not knowing what she was trying to do.

The next thing she heard was the sound of her mother coming in the front door. She had fallen asleep on top of the cloth. She jumped up and rolled the cloth up to hide it. She spun around in her room trying to decide the best place to put it so that mother wouldn't find it. She shoved the cloth into her pillow case until she could safely return it to the magic box.

On Saturday morning Cynder got out to the garden as soon as the sun came up. She decided to repeat the process that brought Gilly in the first place. She put the hose on soaker and sprayed the Gaillardia flowers waiting for Gilly to appear.

"Gilly," she whispered in a loud voice, "Gilly, I need to talk to you."

She soaked the flowers so much that one of the flowers could not stand the weight and the stem snapped right at the base of the flower.

"Oh, I'm sorry," Cynder cried, apologizing to the flower. She dropped the hose and fell to her knees. She held the flower in her hand, trying to figure out how she could mend it. She felt awful that she had broken one of her flowers.

"I was just trying to get Gilly, to come back, I'm so sorry." She stroked the stem and kissed the face of the flower as tears streamed down her face. "I'm sorry."

"You can heal it." Cynder heard a radiant voice sing over her shoulder.

"What?" Cynder asked though her tears as she spun around on her knees. She tried to wipe the tears from her cheek and dirt smeared across her face.

She was expecting to see Gilly but instead saw a life-sized fairy floating just above the ground. Cynder blinked hard again and again trying to clear her eyes of tears.

This fairy was taller than Cynder and was calming and mystical, compared to Gilly, and appeared to be quite a bit older. Her wings were a beautiful blue, starting light blue next to her body then gradually turning darker towards the tips. They had shimmers of gold flecked throughout them. The fairy had wispy brown hair that hung past her waist and shined in the sunlight. She wore a beautiful flowing blue gown that seemed to have a life of its own. Brilliant blue stars adorned the gown as well as her matching blue stockings and arm warmers. Cynder had never seen a sight so spectacular and dazzling in her life. She felt mesmerized in her presence.

"Lazuli," the fairy said, bowing slightly and she pointed a wand towards Cynder. The stone in the wand was deep blue like a night sky and had flecks of gold running through it. Cynder noticed that the stone was the same kind as the one on her necklace. When the fairy waved the wand at Cynder, both her wand and Cynder's stone shimmered and tiny shards of light passed quickly back and forth between them.

This startled Cynder and she instinctively wrapped her fingers around her stone. It heated in her fist.

"Cynder, your stone is Lapis Lazuli as well as my wand. Lapis is one of the most powerful stones and should be used with care. It will help you to confront the truth and accept what that truth teaches you. It is known as the wisdom stone and can help to direct harmony and healing, and stimulate the powers of the mind. Your stone can be used to help you contact spirit guardians and can be used for healing in many areas, for example, it can alleviate pain; purify blood, and sooth autism. You may use it to heal your flower." She motioned the wand towards the flower in Cynder's hand.

"What... how?" Cynder turned her attention to the head of the flower she still held in her hand.

"Lapis Lazuli stone holds great healing energy. When used properly with the right intentions it can promote healing. You have exhibited great compassion, as well as appreciation and caring in the Garden of Lapis, Cynder. You have been the one chosen to use this stone. You will go on to use it in many gardens and will help people as well."

Cynder looked puzzled. She looked from her stone to the flower and then back to the fairy.

"You found the stone in this, the Garden of Lapis," the fairy said sweeping her arm over the garden. "I left it for you a long time ago Cynder."

For the first time in a long time, Cynder didn't mind being called Cynder. When the fairy said 'Cynder' it sounded mystical.

"I did find this stone in the garden a long time ago. My mother had a necklace made out of it," Cynder explained. Her stone was elongated and had a point on the end. She rubbed the stone between her fingers instinctively.

"Take the stone and point it at the flower in your hand, then concentrate as hard as you can in your heart. Think about how much you love and care for this flower. See it in your mind as if it was already restored to its natural beauty."

Cynder thought this was the oddest thing she'd ever heard, but she was willing to give it a try. She pointed the end of her necklace at the flower in her hand. She concentrated on it as hard as she could. The gold in the stone began to swirl and light up, as it had in the wand, and it felt warm. Cynder got scared by it and stopped. She looked up at the fairy.

"Don't be afraid, Cynder. Continue." She pointed her wand, directing Cynder.

Cynder tried again.

The head of the flower shivered and went back into its bud.

Cynder looked at the fairy, "It didn't work," she said. Her shoulders dropped.

"Keep going, refocus with your heart, your heart has … let me say this so that you can understand it." She paused for a moment. "The heart has power tools and one of them is appreciation. So you can use this appreciation through your heart and into the stone to direct energy, or love, you could call it, into where you want healing to happen," the fairy explained to her. "Place the stone on the stem where it is broken, it is your intention that is most important. Think about how much you love this garden and each and every plant in it, and then focus on sending this appreciation into your lapis stone."

Cynder did as she was told and the flower bud vanished from her hand and she was left with a small pile of dust. "It still didn't work," she said and her chin began to quiver.

"Look at the stem my child."

Cynder turned back towards the stem and the bud was intact on the stem. Cynder couldn't believe her eyes. The stem had somehow healed onto the flower bud. She petted the velvety bud as anyone else would pet a new born kitten.

"Oh thank you!" Cynder giggled. "Please tell me who you are?"

Apparently Cynder was starting to get manners.

"My name is Lazuli after the stone. I am the fairy of healing."

"I don't understand. Why is all of this happening to me?"

"It is not for us to question why, Cynder. We must just be grateful for the gifts and talents we are given, and the right to use them."

"What about mom or Aunt Krystal?"

"Your mother was chosen to heal through her massage work and your aunt through her teaching. You were chosen to help special children and flowers in nature. Your love of nature makes you right for this purpose in life. You are lucky Cynder, most people never learn of their purpose in life when they are so young. I must go now, you need to rest."

"Wait," Cynder cried, "can I get you or Gilly to appear with this stone?"

"It's not quite that simple, but practice. I don't want to overwhelm you," Lazuli claimed.

Lazuli waved her wand and a door magically appeared behind her. It opened when she pointed her wand at it and bright blue lights sparkled and flowed out from the opening and surrounded Lazuli, spinning her slowly in a mist until she could be seen no more. The mist pulled back through the door and everything vanished.

Cynder turned back to the flower that had just healed. She was amazed that her Lapis stone could work such miracles. She looked as deeply as she possibly could into her stone. The next thing she knew she was waking up from a nap on the floor of the garden, looking at the stars and hearing the sound of her mother calling her to the house.

Sunday was a day of magic for Jessilyn and Krystal. So, as usual, Cynder was in her garden; the Garden of Lapis. But today she was practicing her own magic- the magic of healing plants in her garden.

She healed flowers, leaves, branches, and she even healed a frog.

Jessilyn brought out the magic box to the kitchen table where Krystal was sitting. She fished through it until she came out with a deck of Tarot cards. She didn't even notice that the fairy cloth was missing from the box.

"What are you hoping to find out this time Jess?" Krystal asked as she removed the cards from the box and handed them to Jessilyn.

"Same old thing," Jessilyn said flatly, "when and where will I meet my knight in shining armor?".

They both laughed.

Jessilyn shuffled the deck and handed it to Krystal, who laid the cards out in special order. She flipped cards and they discussed what came up. Jessilyn asked, "Do you think we'll ever get too old to enjoy reading Tarot cards?"

"Nope," Krystal said, "it's too much fun, plus it gives us an opportunity to spend time together."

"I never used to have anyone to do Tarot with until I met you." She smiled at Krystal. "I started doing them in high school by myself. Did I ever tell you about the voodoo doll that I made?"

"No Jess you didn't," Krystal said and looked up from the cards. "For real?"

"Yes and no," Jessilyn admitted. "I hated this girl in high school, and besides my mother's meddling, she is the other one that ruined my high school life. She came from a very poor family and she stole from everyone. She even tried to steal my boyfriend all through high school. She was a cheerleader with me and it was awful. No one liked her. Well anyway, I made this voodoo doll to be- um…mean I guess." She looked down in shame. "I didn't really know what I was doing, nothing happened to her because of it."

"Wow you were a wicked one," Krystal said.

"Do you want to see it?" Jessilyn asked with a playful grin on her face.

"You still have it?" Krystal whispered.

"Yeah, it's at the bottom of this box. I didn't really know what I was doing though. Remember that when you see it."

Jessilyn rummaged through the box until she got to the bottom. She pulled out the most ridiculous looking thing meant to be a doll. It was more like a little white hankie wrapped around a Popsicle stick, secured with rubber bands, and stuffed with tissues. Jessilyn had taken a pen and drawn a primitive face on it. On the doll's chest she had put a little red heart and stuck a pin through it.

She sat it in the middle of the table.

The rubber bands were dried up and loose, the stuffing was falling out, and it looked more like a mouse nest than a doll.

Krystal was disappointed it wasn't a little more sophisticated.

Jessilyn looked embarrassed by the small mess.

They both stared at the sad little doll lying in the middle of the table.

"Pitiful isn't it," Jessilyn said, "The whole thing is pitiful. I had better get rid of it before Cynder sees it. I wouldn't want to give her any ideas. She'd probably make one that looked like me."

They both laughed. Jessilyn took the doll over to the waste basket and buried it at the bottom.

Jessilyn should have removed the pin from the doll's heart though, because she didn't know what she was doing. She didn't know a damaged heart could cause harm to others.

CHAPTER SEVEN

Until the Pleiades School got more plants, Cynder had nothing to do. Krystal assigned her to observe Grant as he played in the activity room. She was to record what he drew or formed out of the materials in the room. Aunt Krystal was grooming Cynder for working with autistic children. Cynder had no idea what that meant, but she was going to take this opportunity to use her stone the way that Lazuli taught her in the garden.

When no one was looking Cynder bent over Grant so that her necklace was near his head. She pretended she was fiddling with it so that she could point it where she wanted. She concentrated on caring for him and on wishing that he could recognize her. She had her eyes closed and felt heat from her stone. She peeked out at it. Little loops of blue, green, and white light swirled around the stone, forming an aura of light around Grant's head. As the light became brighter, the stone grew warmer. Cynder glanced around the room to see if anyone was watching. No one seemed to notice anything.

She concentrated on her heart and on love and kindness towards Grant. She formed a visional picture of him playing on the beach, as he was in her dream. She pictured herself standing beside him stroking his head. A tiny tornado formed around the oblong stone and jumped off from the tip of the stone onto Grant's head. Cynder heard and felt a quiet snap. It felt like the light shock two people have cross between them when they walk on carpet. Cynder felt excitement in the pit of her stomach but it frightened her a little. She pulled her necklace back and stood upright.

Grant didn't seem to react to it.

Was I imagining this? Cynder began to stroke Grant's head again.

Cynder felt an overwhelming passion she had never felt before. She began to tear up. What just happened? Was it love? Was it healing energy? Or was it just her imagination?

No, Cynder thought, *this is not my imagination.*

Aunt Krystal came in the room and approached Cynder.

Oh no, Cynder thought, *did she see that? Will she make me leave the school?*

"How is Grant doing?" Krystal asked. Apparently she hadn't seen anything unusual.

Grant started drawing stars with crayons. Cynder pointed this out to Aunt Krystal and she showed some interest. Cynder had a pit in her stomach and she felt like she couldn't contain her emotion. She looked down at Grant and blinked away her tears. She gulped in an effort to steady her voice before she spoke. She arched her back and stretched her arms overhead and faked a long yawn, so that she could regain her composure.

She put her hand on Grant's head and played with his curls. "Grant is making beautiful stars Aunt Krystal."

"He doesn't usually let anyone touch him," Krystal said softly. She looked lovingly at Cynder. "I knew you would be good with these children."

Cynder nodded her head, "I am surprised myself, and I didn't know I liked little kids."

"Very nice stars Grant," Aunt Krystal told him. He continued playing, not looking at either one of them. He picked up a new piece of paper and drew a star using one continuous line. Aunt Krystal gasped as she watched.

"I don't believe this," she told Cynder, "drawing any star with a single line is significant for any five year old child, but this is a seven-pointed star. This is a septagram and his drawing a star such as this is an indication of great intelligence. I don't think I could even draw one this nice free handed. We must have him retested." She left the room with the paper studying it closely.

Cynder almost cried again.

Grant pulled out a piece of poster paper and drew another seven pointed star. This time he added three inner lapping circles to the middle of the star.

Cynder had seen this star before; could it be the one on her mother's fairy cloth?

"For Cinderella," he said quietly and handed it to Cynder, glancing into her eyes for only an instant.

Cynder was shocked; this was the first time he had ever acknowledged her when it wasn't a dream…and he called her Cinderella. She got down on her knees so she could be at his level and gave him a hug.

"Thank you Grant," she told him. "May I keep this?"

He didn't answer her; he dropped his arms to his side and walked away to play with the sand. She took this as a 'yes' and rolled it up and tucked it into her backpack before anyone else could see it. She didn't know if she was allowed to take it, but Cynder didn't always follow the rules.

In the car on the way home that day Cynder was smiling.

"Cynder you never smile. What's up?" Sheridan asked.

"Don't tell…" she said, and turned towards him. "Grant made me a picture."

"How do you know he made it for you?"

"He handed it to me, 'For Cinderella,' he said to me."

"Are you sure? Mom says he doesn't talk. What is this Cinderella stuff anyways? You don't ever let anyone call you that."

"Well she's wrong, he can talk." She was acting smug with him. "It's a long story, I may tell you someday," Cynder said. She grasped her backpack a little tighter.

"You're the weirdest girl I know Cynthia."

"Oh you can call me Cynder."

Sheridan shook his head, "I'll never understand women," he said.

CYNDER

CHAPTER EIGHT

Cynder went into the house to change into an older white dress and took the chance to pull the Fairy cloth from her pillow case. She compared it to the star that Grant drew her. Yes, it was definitely a fairy star that he had drawn. Cynder got out a pen from her backpack. On Grant's drawing she marked the parts of the fairy star.

She wrote on the inner lapping circles in the middle of the star: 'Body/Earth/Energy,' 'Heaven/Sky/Energy,' and 'Spirit/Self/Energy.' Where they over-lapped she wrote 'Dreams/Energy - Fairy Land in between.'

Cynder took this opportunity to return her mother's fairy cloth to her room before she got home. She rolled up her own picture that Grant made her and put it into her backpack to take out to the garden with her. Her mother never came into the garden, so she knew that she was safe to look at it out there.

Cynder climbed up into a tree with her backpack. She got out her new fairy star drawing and spread it out on a large limb and studied it.

Out of nowhere, Gilly appeared and started speaking from over Cynder's shoulder, right next to her ear. "You finally found your mother's map," Gilly said.

Startled by the sound of Gilly's voice, Cynder jerked and nearly fell out of the tree. When she reached for a branch to hold her balance, the fairy star picture floated to the ground.

"You need to warn me next time you pop in like that," Cynder snapped, trying to regain her balance.

Gilly laughed. "Oh, nice to see you too, I thought you wanted me to come back?" She flew in front of Cynder's face.

"Well, I did," said Cynder. "But I almost fell out of a tree. You need to be more careful with that magic stuff that you have."

"I could leave," Gilly said, pointing to the sky, "but I thought I'd tell you a little bit about that map."

"It's a map?" Cynder asked, "Tell me what you know about it."

Gilly dove towards the map.

Cynder dropped out of the tree to try to beat her down. Of course, this was impossible. Humans, even dropping out of the sky, cannot outdo fairies zipping and zapping about.

"Did you notice that those three circles inside all have the word 'energy' in the description?"

"I did notice 'energy,'" said Cynder. She caught up with Gilly and plopped beside her. "What does it mean?"

"It means that all of these areas can inner-lap through energy, because everything has energy. You have energy, I have energy, love is energy, light is energy, and thoughts are energy." Gilly was buzzing around the map and speaking excitedly. "This is what makes it so that I can go back and forth between fairyland, Earth, and even your dreams. Anyone can learn to walk around in their own dreams and make them what they want them to be." She tapped her finger on Cynder's head. "And other people can walk around in your dreams, your waking dreams, and your sleeping dreams too. It's like magic."

"You mean how Grant has been in my dreams … that kind of energy and you're saying that energy has no boundaries?"

"That's right it has no boundaries and it can walk through our minds and though doors. It knows no time, so past, present and future do not exist separately. Energy takes no permanent shape and is ever changing."

"So," Cynder said, "everything exists at the same time and we can change it."

"Yes exactly. Everyone has the power to use it like that. It's really a possibility you see, and dreaming is really waking up. Our dreams are powerful and we can learn a lot from them if we listen to them. It's not magic in the way that humans think of magic. It's not trickery. It's not a secret. It's being open to the thought of using your dream information the same way you use your 'awake' information."

"So I really need to pay more attention to my dreams," Cynder said. "And I shouldn't dismiss them as something that is happening 'to' me but something that is happening 'for' me, so that I can use the information to learn from, or use it to help me in some way." Cynder was beginning to make sense of it all.

"Yes," said Gilly, "your lapis stone helps your dream work and your healing. And I think Lazuli told you that healing is the intention of giving and accepting love, and the ability to heal comes through caring about those you know, and those you don't know, and those you hope to know someday." Gilly lay down on the map and curled up. "Teaching is exhausting. I need to take a nap." She closed her eyes.

"No, Gilly, wake up, I'm just beginning to catch on, I want to know more," Cynder said. She was excited to be learning all of these new things. "Today I think I healed Grant a little bit. He's the one that drew this star. This isn't my mother's fairy cloth. I just wrote the words on it. Grant drew the star and the inner lapping circles. Drawing a septagram is a sign of high intelligence for a boy that age." Cynder could not have been more proud quoting her Aunt Krystal.

"You're catching on faster than your mother did," Gilly mumbled. She lay with her eyes closed.

"My mother worked with you like I do?" This surprised Cynder.

"Yes and she was even more stubborn than you are." Gilly rolled over and looked at Cynder. "She closed herself off to us a very long time ago. I didn't think that you would catch on so fast."

"Why would you think that?" Cynder asked. She took offense to the remark.

Gilly sat up. "Well you seem set in your ways, very stubborn about things… like that white dress." Gilly said. She scrunched her face and tilted her head to the side. "And it seems like you don't like people very much."

"Did you ever think that maybe people don't like me?"

"You can say whatever you want," Gilly said. She slid back down on her side. "But I see what goes on. If you don't try to get along with others, they're not going try to get along with you. I must say, I'm really glad to see that you're helping Grant. He's a very special boy. And you'll find out just how special someday."

"I was really happy today when I could help him. I mean, I think I helped him."

"I happen to know that you did." Gilly rolled over on her back and drew her hands behind her head.

"So, before you just disappear on me again," Cynder said, "how can I get you to come here when I want to talk to you?"

Gilly sat up. "That's a harder one to help you with, because sometimes I'm out doing things at other places for other people, or fairies, or nature spirits. You don't know anything about them yet."

"Nature spirits?" Cynder said. She realized there was so much more for her to learn.

"Yeah, I think that's enough teaching for today, I'm tired. I don't want to overwhelm you. But I can tell you if you come to the garden, and just relax and think about me, sometimes I'll come around, if I'm available. And sometimes I'll just pop in unexpectedly like I did today. You don't really have any control over that. It's really that way with all the fairies, and nature spirits, we hear you seeking us, but you don't really have any control over us. But if you put us in your thoughts, then you have a better chance of getting us."

"Okay but, go back to this map for a minute, the seven points, they must stand for something. Could you just tell me about that before you leave?"

"They are the seven magical elements you see and each one has a direction, the seven are; Earth-North, Air-East, Fire-South, Water-West, Life-Above, Light-Below, and the last one is for Magic- and the direction is Within. Remember though, magic, energy, and healing are a part of everything. The number seven is important in many ways too. However, make no mistake that healing is always one part energy and two parts love. And remember, that everyone has energy, but sometimes the love is a little more difficult to give out."

Cynder nodded her head and drew her focus more into the map. "And this here...what is that?" She turned in the direction where Gilly lay.

Gilly was standing straight up with her arms tight to her sides. She lit up and was going off like a Fourth of July sparkler, and when it burnt out completely, she was gone.

Cynder got out a pen from her backpack and wrote the new information on the points of the star as Gilly had described them. She also wrote on the bottom of the paper: healing = one part energy, two parts love.

CYNDER

CHAPTER NINE

Friday finally came and when Cynder got to the Pleiades that day she and Sheridan were approached by two people. One was a high school girl who looped her arm around Sheridan's and told him that she was working with him today. His face turned red and he smiled at her. "Great," he said. They turned and walked off.

The second one approached Cynder. He was a very old gentleman, at least 80, dressed in clothes at least 100 years old, Cynder thought. He introduced himself as Ed and he had a grand smile. He had a lot of wrinkles, but Cynder could see dimples in his cheeks when he smiled, that gave him the appearance of being younger. His brilliant blue eyes stood out on his tanned skin. He was tall and thin and looked like he didn't get enough to eat. Cynder thought that he looked like a farmer, due to his overalls.

Ed explained that he was instructed by Krystal to take young Cynder wherever she wanted to go to purchase flowers and to allow her to get anything that she thought the Pleiades would need to look spectacular.

Cynder was glad that he didn't try to loop his arm through hers as that girl had to Sheridan.

Cynder followed him to a rickety old flatbed truck. At first she was put off by the appearance of both him and the truck, she was embarrassed to be seen with him and a little bit scared. But then she realized that this was her ticket to whatever flower nursery she wanted to go to, so she thought it might be a chance to find her father.

She thought Ed must be very poor and maybe had no place to wash his clothes. They were stained and torn at both knees and the right elbow. His cap was so faded Cynder couldn't read the writing on it. One of his boots even had a hole in the toe.

His truck was so rusty that you couldn't tell what color it was supposed to be or exactly what was holding it together. She looked around the truck and quarter-sized lumps of rust were scattered all over the driveway. Cynder felt sorry for him. She was glad that he didn't smell.

Ed opened her door for her. The truck appeared to be in pain from being opened, because the hinges on the door groaned and the door deposited more rust on the ground. When Cynder pulled herself up into the worn seat it felt springy.

The first thing she wanted to do right from the start was get him clear on her name. She needed him to call her Cynthia. Cynder was too uncommon a name for her to be introduced as, just in case she found her father today, she didn't want him to know it was her until she was ready.

"Why?" Ed said. "I did like the name, Cynder; I never met a Cynder before." He put the keys in the ignition, shrugged his shoulders, and said, "But I'm told you're the boss, and that's okay with me, Cynthia. Where to?"

Ed wrapped his gnarled old fingers around the steering wheel. He cranked up the engine and stomped his foot on the gas pedal twenty times, at least. A big puff of black smoke rolled out from behind the truck. The truck shook, and heaved, and coughed like a cat trying to get rid of a fur-ball. Cynder ducked low, hoping no one would see her. The truck rattled down the long driveway and was as loud as train.

"There's a nursery on the outskirts of town. Do you know about it?" Cynder shouted. She had no idea of its location, and hoped Ed did.

"I know of two, which one you want to see?" he shouted back.

"The one that makes pottery," Cynder said.

Ed stopped the truck. "I know of one that does."

Ed pulled out onto the road. "We have all day. Let's go check it out." He floored the old truck, which spit and popped, but really didn't change its speed much.

It seemed, to Cynder, like they drove and drove forever, but Ed said they only went 10 miles from the center of town. Maybe it just felt like a long time because Cynder felt nervous. The truck had one speed and that was slow. She had no idea where they were. She played with her necklace to help steady her nerves.

So many questions came to mind that she felt like her head was a popcorn popper. *What would I say to my father if this was his place? Would I be able to talk to him at all? Would I get mad at him because he didn't try harder to find me?* She really didn't need to say anything to him today about who she was. She had to make sure it was him in the first place.

When they finally came upon it, Ed pulled into the driveway. The sign out front said 'Landscapes of Eden.' The buildings were quite a ways off from the road and all of the plants, greenhouses, and outbuildings were behind the house. It seemed to take forever for the old truck to crawl down that long driveway.

Cynder was excited, but scared and nervous at the same time; she began to bite at her lower lip. She didn't know what to expect. *Will he be able to tell that I am his daughter? Do I look like him? Will he be tall and handsome? Will he be a nice person?*

She grasped the stone from her necklace and hoped he was everything she'd wanted in a father.

"You go pick out the flowers you want," Ed told her, "and I'll go find the owner and make arrangements for everything to get billed to the Pleiades."

Cynder tried to focus on the flowers, but she was curious to see the man who owned the place. She walked through the rows of beautiful flowers; always keeping a watchful eye on where Ed had stepped into a large building, a lean-to, on the back of the house. After a few minutes Ed returned. The pleasant look he had on his face a moment ago was gone. He looked like he had seen a monster in that building. Beads of sweat formed on his face.

"What did you find out?" Cynder inquired. She felt more nervous than she ever had in her life.

"She said we could take a look around."

"She?" Cynder probed, "the owner is a she?"

"No, she's not," he grumbled, "she just likes to think she's the owner." He pulled off his hat and scratched the back of his head making his thick gray hair stick out. "Looks like she's packing up." He shook his head, and plopped his hat back on. "Cynthia I'm not real sure what she's doing here. I think maybe we should go back to the school for the day."

"Oh, no," Cynder said, "I see some plants here that are rare." She made this up, because she didn't want to leave. "I need to talk to the owner about them."

"Alright," Ed said. He took a rumpled, red bandana out of his pocket and wiped the back of his neck and then his face.

They walked around for about five minutes and Cynder let him know first-hand how much she knew about gardening by naming several plants, flowers, and soils, watering needs, sunshine and shade conditions. She told him which plants would be best for indoor or outdoor planting.

"You sure do know a lot about gardening for such a young girl. How did you learn so much?"

"Internet," she replied. In fact, Cynder went to a website

to help her learn about the area of healing at:
acenterforsuccess.com she liked to look up new things on the
internet now, and found that there was a lot to learn about
healing.

He nodded. "Do you see anything you like here?"

"Yes," Cynder said, "maybe- maybe you're right, maybe
we should we go someplace else? I mean if the owner's not
here."

"Well I-," he stopped abruptly. He scratched his chin and
focused back towards the house. "Here she comes now."

A small woman with short black hair headed their way,
and she looked like she was in a big hurry. She was not all
that cordial upon her approach and she ignored Cynder
completely.

"I need to leave. Come back on Monday." The woman
snapped at Ed, shuffling a heavy box from one hip to the
next.

Ed took a step back from her and pointed to Cynder. "If
she wants," he said, his voice was meek and mild. "She's the
boss."

Cynder couldn't figure out why Ed was acting afraid of
her.

Cynder straightened herself up and stepped forward, even
though she was still taller than this woman without doing so.
"Will the owner be here today?" Cynder asked. She asserted
herself and looked down her nose at the woman.

"Well yes," the woman said, again addressing Ed, "of course he'll be back today." She was oblivious to the fact that Cynder asked the question.

"And what's his name?" Cynder insisted. She stepped between the woman and Ed.

The woman stepped over so that she could see Ed and again she addressed him when she answered. "Jake, of course." She looked puzzled. "Go now." she insisted. She turned and headed for her car.

Cynder rolled her eyes and she and Ed slowly made their way back to the truck.

"You sure are a direct young lady," Ed said. He smirked.

"I like to know what's going on," Cynder said.

"We could go someplace else," he offered.

"No," Cynder insisted, "even though she's mean, it is no reason to take it out on Jake, who apparently *is* the owner."

As they drove away Ed promised her they would go out there again first thing Monday morning and they made arrangements to meet at the school.

Cynder had trouble hiding her excitement on the way back to the school. She felt sure that Jake was 'J' and her father. She was almost giddy and couldn't stop smiling. She kept wiggling in her seat.

"You must really like those plants you saw," Ed said.

"Oh, yeah, the plants," Cynder said biting her lip. "Well I

like that place, you know. It has so much going on there, flowers, plants, and pottery, and so much variety to choose from. I felt comfortable there, and Jake must be a good gardener."

"Comfortable? Around that woman…how could you feel comfortable around her?"

"Well, not her really, just the place," Cynder said. "She didn't seem very nice."

Cynder was so excited about everything that she had to tell Sheridan. She decided that on the way home she would tell him about the letter and her father.

When they returned to the school Cynder saw Sheridan just getting into his car. She thanked Ed for taking her out there and ran to Sheridan with a big smile on her face.

"Not leaving without me are you?" she shouted across the parking lot.

"No of course not," Sheridan said. He swung the back door open and waved her in. "Hop in."

"Funny," Cynder said. "You know I always ride shot-gun."

"Someone beat you to it," he said. He smiled and bent over, glancing to the shot-gun position in the front passenger seat. When he saw the look on Cynder's face his gaze fell to his feet and his smile dropped completely from his face.

To Cynder this was a big insult. "Who is that in my seat?" Cynder whispered.

"Her name is Basha," Sheridan said.

"What's 'a Basha'?" Cynder said, narrowing her eyes and folding her arms in front of her.

"Don't be rude, Cynder. I met her today at the school. We worked together all day. She goes to my high school and I'm giving her a ride home. I'll drop you off first, hop in." He waved his arm again trying to get her to get in.

Cynder realized that this was the girl who had looped her arm through Sheridan's this morning. She huffed as loudly as she could and threw herself into the back seat. Sheridan made brief introductions, but Cynder was not too friendly.

She pulled out her headphones, which she hardly ever used. She listened to their conversation. The drool voice of Basha, as she flirted with Sheridan on the way home, made Cynder feel awkward and sick to her stomach.

Each time Sheridan looked at Cynder in the rear view mirror she narrowed her eyes at him.

Basha was continually texting her friends on the ride and told Sheridan he should get a cell phone so that they could text each other. Sheridan quickly glanced in the rear view mirror and Cynder rolled her eyes.

The normally enjoyable short ride, was painful and long for Cynder. As they neared her driveway she bit her lip to keep herself from saying something hurtful to both of them.

"Drop me off out here," Cynder demanded before he turned in her drive.

"Are you sure Cynder?" Sheridan asked. He stopped the car.

She jumped out of the car and started down her drive without saying a word to them.

"I'll pick you up on Monday," Sheridan hollered at her.

With her back to him she gestured a dismissive 'whatever' wave to him.

CHAPTER TEN

Cynder couldn't wait to get out to her garden. She grabbed a trowel from the garden shed and worked the dirt. She pulled feverously at any weed that she could find, jerking one out by the roots. She spoke to it, "I don't want you here Basha." She threw it over her shoulder and pulled another one. "I don't need you here Basha." This one went flying. "I need to get rid of you," she said to another weed jabbing her trowel deep into its roots.

"What's 'a Basha'?" Gilly asked appearing out of thin air. She buzzed around Cynder's head.

"As if you don't know," Cynder said. She whipped a weed at Gilly, who zig-zagged just in time to miss it.

Gilly flipped in the air and then landed in a seated position on Cynder's shoulder. She giggled. "Bet you didn't know I could do that. Sorry for picking on you, I know you've had an eventful day."

"You can say that again." Cynder gently picked Gilly up from her shoulder and held her in the palm of her hand in front of her face. "So is this Jake my father?"

"What does your gut tell you?"

"My gut tells me he is. What else can you tell me about him?"

"Well…" Gilly said, her eyes glistening…

Cynder's eyes were so fixed on Gilly that she wasn't aware that Lazuli was towering behind her.

Gilly's gaze went above Cynder's head and the lively expression disappeared from her face. Gilly snapped her fingers and she was gone, just like that. No announcement that she was leaving, no fancy exit, just a snap and then nothing. No lights, no bells, no whistles, and no sparklers or fireworks.

"Good afternoon Cynder," Lazuli sang.

Cynder turned around slowly. "Can you two not be in the same place at the same time?"

Lazuli floated magically in front of Cynder. She looked like a reflection in the water. "That's not it Cynder. Gilly needs to let you work out some of these things on your own and not give you the answers to everything. Sometimes she forgets that she's a fairy not a human. We fairies help differently than humans do. You should go to your mother with some of the questions you wish Gilly to answer."

"I can't talk to my mother, she's very difficult." Cynder

moaned.

"Are you sure that you aren't the difficult one and you make your mother seem difficult?" Lazuli reasoned.

Cynder put her hand up defensively. "She never wants to talk about anything with me."

"Have you considered that it might be painful for your mother to talk about your father and your grandmother?"

"No, I guess I never looked at it that way," Cynder said, looking down at the flowerbed.

"There is a reason that she left this town and there is a reason that she came back when she did," Lazuli explained.

"What are those reasons?" Cynder begged to know.

"They are many and I cannot tell you Cynder. You must discover them yourself." Lazuli crossed her wand over Cynder causing her hair to feel prickly.

"I guess I could ask Aunt Krystal," Cynder proposed.

"Krystal does not possess this knowledge. Your mother has carried these secrets deep inside and has not shared them with anyone. You must find a way to talk to your mother." Lazuli pointed the wand at Cynder as though she were giving an order. The wand shimmered and Cynder's stone snapped. Cynder brought her hand to her stone to feel the energy.

"I wouldn't know where to start." Cynder confessed.

"Start where you began," Lazuli said.

"What does that mean?"

"I know you will figure it out." Lazuli turned and left peacefully through her mystical door.

Cynder stood in her bedroom trying to solve the puzzle. "Start where you began," she whispered Lazuli's orders. She walked over to her fairy statues and held the one that looked most like Lazuli. "Start where I began? What does that mean?"

She took the statue to her desk and ran ideas by her pretend Lazuli. "When I began working in the garden? No, that's not it. When I began school? No. When I began living? Yes, perhaps when I was born."

She pulled open the drawer on her desk and pushed papers and desk junk around until she finally found that special object she was looking for. It was a baby picture that Aunt Krystal had taken of Cynder and Jessilyn in the hospital when she was born. "Here it is," Cynder said with pride.

The little frame, having been in Cynder's possession, was now chipped and dented. In the picture Jessilyn looked lovingly into Cynder's tiny round face that peeked out from a blanket. Cynder couldn't remember a time when her mother looked at her like that.

Mother must have more pictures someplace, she thought. *If there were any, they would be in the attic.* Her mother didn't go into the attic much so Cynder felt free to explore.

Cynder had never ventured into the attic much in the three years that they had lived here. After finding her grandmother's cremation urn with her ashes up there last week, she figured there were other secrets there too.

Jessilyn was in the kitchen making dinner. Cynder knew she had a little while to look around. There were no lights in the narrow stairway to the attic. She crept up the stairs with her flashlight in hand. At the top of the stairs she came face to face with a small doorway. She ducked down and poked her head into the small opening of the attic and paused.

She wondered, *What is it about the attic that makes me feel so afraid? Is it because it is getting dark outside and the attic will be even darker? Is it because the lighting is so bad? Is it because it is so dusty? Is it because it smells? Or is it because this is where mother keeps all of the things that grandmother left behind when she died?*

Cynder had to be brave when she stepped inside the attic.

Shining the flashlight towards the ceiling, Cynder looked for the pull string attached to the light. She stepped towards the string as it dangled down and the door slapped shut. Startled, she swiveled around and caught a stack of boxes with her elbow, knocking the flashlight out of her hand and sending the boxes crashing to the floor.

Cynder sat for a moment waiting for the dust to settle. She couldn't see her flashlight and figured that she broke it when she dropped it.

She crawled through the spilled contents of the boxes that were underneath the light's pull string. She could barely make it out by the faint light from the small window in the attic. She slowly stood. Whatever she was standing on made her slip and slide all over the place as though she were standing on ice. She was finally able to reach up and pull the string.

She looked down and found herself standing in a pile of old letters, and loose photos. The letters were addressed to her grandmother and had the return addresses of several of her mother's homes in Texas. Tucked inside the envelopes were pictures of Cynder from when she was a baby and on into toddlerhood and then her as a young girl. Some of the older envelopes had crayon scribbling on them and what looked like Cynder's effort to write her name or draw. Cynder smiled and stacked these together.

She put them over by the door so that she could take them to her room. *Mother must have sent these to my grandmother.*

The loose photos were her grandmother's collections of photos that didn't make it into albums. There were old black and white ones that Cynder assumed were of her grandmother with her parents, brothers, and sisters, friends, pictures of homes, pets, and cars. The color photos were of Jessilyn growing up.

She found one small album that held nothing but Cynder's grade school pictures. Cynder looked on the backs of some of the pictures and saw that someone had put her name and grade on them. She put this album by the door to take with her.

Then she came to a photo that surprised her. It was of her with an older woman she didn't recognize. On the back of the picture was written 'Grandma and Cynder-age two.'

Cynder was confused; she thought she had never met her grandmother. But here was proof that she had. She tucked the picture into a pocket in her dress. She was not going to misplace this picture. She was upset that her mother had lied to her. She started to cry.

Cynder stood over the pictures. She began to feel like she couldn't breathe. She felt closed in and had to get out of there.

She found a box that had tipped over and was now empty. She carefully placed her chosen collection of pictures, letters, and the album into the box.

She heard her mother call her for dinner. She set the box outside the attic on the first step. She left the light on so that she could find her way when she was ready to go up there again. She began to come down the steps. Her mother called again.

"I'm coming," Cynder hollered. "I need to go wash my hands. I'll be there in a minute."

Cynder needed a minute to put the box in her bedroom and get herself together. After dropping off the box, she went into the bathroom. When she looked in the mirror she saw tear tracks down her cheeks where tears had streamed down her dusty face. She studied her face in the mirror. "Do I look like you grandmother? I didn't know that you met me. Why weren't you in my life?"

"Come on, dinner's getting cold," Jessilyn called.

Cynder washed her face and hands. She was shaking

when she left the bathroom. She bit her lip to keep it from quivering and she slipped into her seat at the table.

"Wow," Jessilyn said, "washing your hands before you come to dinner. I thank you for that."

Jessilyn piled food onto her plate and then handed the dish to Cynder who sat, dumbfounded staring down at her empty plate.

"Are you okay," Jessilyn asked when Cynder didn't take the dish.

Cynder turned away to gather her thoughts. She turned back to her mother and opened her mouth to speak but her words were stuck in her head.

"Cynder are you okay? Are you hungry?"

Cynder sighed deeply. "Am I hungry?" Cynder said quietly and paused. She picked up her napkin and sat it on her lap, avoiding eye contact with her mother. "Um…no, I'm… I'm not. I want to go to my room." Cynder sat staring at her plate. She made no effort to leave the table.

"Are you sick?" Her mother asked. She couldn't tell from Cynder's face that she was sick.

Cynder stared blankly at her mother. She wanted to scream at her. She was confused. She was angry. She wanted to know why she didn't let her spend time with her grandmother when she was old enough to remember it and before she died. Cynder placed her napkin over her mouth to hold in all of her hurt feelings and her many questions. She wondered why her mother kept so many things a secret from her; her father, her grandmother, her very own history. She wasn't ready to confront her yet. Tears began to well up in her eyes.

Cynder stood and threw her napkin on her plate. "I may be sick. I need to lie down."

Jessilyn, who could never tune into Cynder's thoughts or feelings, shrugged her shoulders. "Well, I hope I don't catch anything from you, I need to work tomorrow."

Cynder's head flinched back. "I'm sure it's nothing you could catch," she said as she fled from the room.

A person can't catch feelings. A person can't catch confusion. And a person can't understand what her only daughter thinks of her, Cynder screamed inside her head as she hurried to her room.

CYNDER

CHAPTER ELEVEN

Cynder had trouble falling asleep that evening. When she finally did she was at the beach again. The pictures that she had seen in the attic that day were now washing up on the shore of her dream. She sat on the edge of the water in the sand watching them rush in and slowly float out, in and out, over and over again.

Grant came into the dream after awhile. He took a seat next to her. He had a fairy statue in his hand and he gave it to her. The young fairy was dressed in dark green colored overalls, had translucent green wings, and was curled up and sleeping in a nest of brown twigs and green leaves. It wore a tiny wreath of blue flowers around its head. "Thank you Grant," she said, and put her hand on his head.

He laid his head on her lap. She slowly brushed her fingers through his hair. "I'm healing," he said sweetly, "Cinderella, I'm healing."

Cynder cried. In the dream state she couldn't pinpoint what she was crying about. It was a happy and a sad cry at the same time. She said, "I'm confused, I'm so confused."

She was coming out of her sleep when she saw her mother in her room hanging up a clean dress on the back of her door.

" Confused?" her mother said, "You only have white dresses to choose from." She walked back out into the hall. "I'm off to work."

Cynder took a long 'wake-up' stretch in her bed. She glanced up at the shelf of fairies. She noticed something different on one of the shelves. "What the heck?" She jumped out of bed. The fairy that Grant had given her in the dream was now sitting on her shelf. She was almost afraid to pick it up for fear that it was just in her imagination and would disappear if she touched it. She slowly reached for it, laying one finger on it gently. "Yep, it's real," she whispered. She picked it up and found that it was heavier than a lot of her other fairies. Then she noticed that it was not a girl fairy, it was a boy. Its hair was similar to Grant's and the face looked like him. She ran her hands gently across it and put it next to the statue that looked like her.

Cynder wanted to get out of the house; she needed a break from her emotions, and all of the pictures. All she wanted to do was work in the garden with her flowers. She wanted her old life back, she wanted to be the old Cynder, and she didn't want to feel all this pain and confusion. She never used to cry like this.

She pulled the hose around to water the flowers, being real careful not to over soak or break any flowers so that no fairies would appear or come running to their rescue.

An hour had gone by and Cynder had worked with her flowers and was able to put a lot of her emotions away for a little while at least.

Cynder looked up and saw Sheridan at the gate. She didn't know how long he had been standing there. He wasn't trying to get in but instead just stood there. He looked so handsome and grown-up. Cynder never noticed before how good looking he was.

Cynder looked back down at the flowers and watched the water run on them. Her heart was racing a little. She thought it was because she was still angry with him.

"May I ... May I come in Cynder?" he asked.

"Do what you want," Cynder snapped.

"I can't understand why you're so mad about a little thing like someone else riding in the shot-gun seat."

"You just don't get it." Of course, Cynder didn't get it either. She couldn't understand why she was so mad at him. It wasn't like she liked him in that way. He was like a brother to her. He was older; and he'd liked other girls before.

"You'd like Basha, she's real nice. She's in the car. I can go get her."

Cynder threw the hose down. "This is my garden Sheridan; you don't bring anyone in my garden, especially not 'a Basha'."

Sheridan giggled and put his hand up near his mouth to try to stifle it. "Her name is Basha; she is not 'a Basha'." His cell phone rang; he pulled it out of his pocket and looked at it. "It's her."

"Just leave me alone Sheridan. I want to be left alone. You can take your new cell phone and 'your Basha' and leave me alone."

"I don't get you Cynder. Call me when you grow up."

Cynder turned her back on him and began walking towards the back of the garden. She heard the closing of the gate, then the slam of his car door, and then she heard him pull away.

Cynder decided she needed to get some answers from her mother and now was just as good a time as any other.

When she walked into the kitchen her mother was putting groceries away.

"Mom, I… I…" she stammered, "I found some pictures in the attic."

"Oh, who are they of?"

"Me and grandma, I think…" Cynder pulled the picture

from her pocket and laid it on the kitchen table.

"Yes that's of you and grandma." She flipped the picture over. "See, it says so on the back." She turned back around to put the cans in the cupboard.

"But you said I didn't know grandma," Cynder said. She snatched the picture off from the table and returned it to her pocket.

Her mother swiveled around quickly. She shrugged her shoulders. "Well, you wouldn't have remembered her; it had been so long since you'd seen her, so you didn't really know her."

Cynder couldn't believe she was acting so casual. "Why wouldn't you let me see her?"

"It's not my fault Cynder. She didn't want to see you." Jessilyn turned her back to Cynder and stood at the sink. "She came to Texas to see you for awhile, but then quit coming."

"Why did she quit coming?" Cynder asked quickly.

"It's a long story, you wouldn't understand." She shook her head back and forth.

"Let me try to understand Mother." Cynder was growing angry.

"I'm really not ready to talk about this Cynder." She sighed deeply.

"Will you ever be ready?"

"I have been trying to get ready for this discussion." She

turned back around and tears streamed down her face. "You are probably lucky you didn't know my mother. You have no idea what she has done to us."

Cynder softened, "What did she do Mom?"

"It goes back many years-" Jessilyn stopped talking when there was a knock at the door. "Oh that's my date Cynder. We'll have to discuss this later. Could you let him in while I go fix my makeup?"

Jessilyn turned and left the room, leaving Cynder more confused than she was before. *How could she just drop a conversation like this so easily?*

The next day Cynder approached her mom to talk again. Jessilyn walked into the room and tried to walk back out when she saw Cynder at the table.

"Mom stop," Cynder demanded. "We need to finish our conversation from last night."

"Oh, not today Cynder. My blind date didn't go so well. He asked me if I was a witch. Like a person can't wear black and have long hair without being a witch."

"Are you a witch?"

"Seriously Cynder, I don't find that funny."

"In addition to the hair and the black clothes, there is the magic box, and all of the secrets, and-"

"The secret about your grandma is that she didn't approve of me and your father." Jessilyn fell into tears. "Your grandma put a stop to it. She ruined it for us Cynder. We should have been with him; we were so much in love. She was awful to me Cynder, you'll never understand. She didn't want to see you anymore because she found out who your father was." Jessilyn fled the room crying and went to her room and slammed the door.

Cynder felt bad for being so hard on her. Jessilyn never did date much and now she was trying so hard. She told Cynder that she was trying to find her a father. She seemed to be upset all of the time lately.

Cynder couldn't understand how a grandmother could turn her own granddaughter away because she didn't like her father. What could be so bad about him that she didn't like him? Cynder had to know what it was, good or bad, she had to know.

She needed to get a ride out to the landscaping place today. Cynder went to the phone and called Sheridan.

"You were mad at me yesterday, Cynder. Now you want a ride?" Sheridan said when she asked him the favor.

"I forgive you. Can you give me a ride?"

"Forgive me for what?" he asked.

"Listen Sheridan if you don't want to give me a ride, I

guess I can ride my bike, but to go there and back it would be more than 20 miles in one day. I can't ride my bike that far. But I guess if you won't give me a ride…" She hoped she could get him to feel sorry for her.

"I'll be right over, bye."

Sheridan pulled into the driveway and Cynder ran out to the car. She didn't want her mother to know where she was going.

"Why do you need to go out there on a Sunday? They probably won't even be open," he said.

"I want to look at some of the plants for Ed to buy tomorrow. I want to take my time picking them out. I don't want to make Ed wait." Cynder didn't know she could make up lies so easily.

"Okay then let's go."

They made small talk about their volunteer jobs. Cynder avoided talking about her mother and their fight and Sheridan avoided talking about Basha.

They pulled into the drive and they could see a moving van parked beside the house. Cynder began to worry. If 'J' moves she might never be able to find him again. She felt she had to go up to the place and convince him to stay.

"It looks like they're busy. You can go tomorrow with Ed," Sheridan said.

"I want to go for a minute Sheridan, I won't bother them."

Sheridan hesitated but drove her back towards the house. Cynder told him to stay in the car and she would find out if they were open. Of course, all she was looking for was Jake. Cynder trembled as she went to the back of the van. Of the three men loading the van, none of them was Jake. The woman that was there the other day wasn't around either. The movers told Cynder that the owners had left for the day.

Cynder went back to Sheridan's car. She was visibly upset. "It's closed." She slumped down in the shot-gun seat.

"What's wrong Cynder?"

Cynder had to lie again. She hated lying to Sheridan. "I just wanted to get out of the house. I was fighting with my mom."

"I don't know why you two can't get along."

She sat up in her seat. "Sheridan, has your mom ever mentioned my father?"

"I asked one time and mom said Jessilyn wouldn't even tell her. I let it go."

"I need to find out who he is Sheridan. I can't let it go."

"Is that what you and your mom are fighting about?"

"Yeah, it's more than my clothes or my hair this time." Cynder said. "Do you want to help me find him?"

"I can't do that to my mom Cynder," he said, "I don't

think she'd want me involved."

"Chicken?" Cynder accused him.

"I don't fight with my mom like that. If your mom won't tell you, it would be impossible to find him."

"I believe he's closer than you think." Cynder gave him a sly smile.

That evening Cynder went into a dream state. She was walking among the plants and flowers at the Landscapes of Eden. This dream felt different. She was in control this time and guided herself where she wanted to go. It was almost like she was awake, yet she knew she was dreaming.

She recognized the plants and flowers she had seen before. She bent over to cup a flower bud, but she couldn't grasp it. She tried again without success. It was like she had the physical properties of a ghost.

She looked up at the house where she knew Jake was sleeping. She was tempted, but afraid, to go into the house. She wondered if anyone would be able to see her.

Maybe I'll just peek into the window...

She turned to walk toward his house, but before she got there she woke up in her own room. Daylight was shining through her window. *That was an interesting way to dream. I need to practice that.*

CHAPTER TWELVE

Cynder arrived at the school the next morning excited to find Ed and go out to the Landscapes of Eden. She noticed his truck parked out front but he wasn't in it. She saw a woman sitting in a red sports car watching the school. She walked towards it and noticed that it was the woman from the landscaping place. She thought this woman may be looking for her.

When she got about ten feet from the car, the woman threw the car into gear, floored the gas, and sent the car into fish-tails. Tiny bits of gravel spun off from the tires striking Cynder in her legs. The car roared out of the drive of the Pleiades leaving a trail of dust behind it.

That was strange, reasoned Cynder, *I must tell Ed about it.*

When she didn't find him out front she charged inside the

school looking for him. No one seemed to know where he was. The people in the office told her to find Krystal; she always knew where everybody was.

She went to Grant's room first, because that is where Krystal spent a lot of her time working with the young teacher assigned to that room. She saw Basha sitting next to the sandbox watching Grant. Basha looked up and grimaced at Cynder.

Grant was building a sandcastle. The castle was a foot and a half tall. This was an improvement from the one story bucket castles he had been attempting to build when Cynder first met him.

Grant saw Cynder look into the room. "Cinderella, Cinderella," he chanted as he ran towards her and wrapped himself around her leg.

Cynder tousled Grant's hair. Cynder watched as Basha took a shovel and shoved the sandcastle over. Basha glared at Cynder with a smug smile on her face when she'd flattened it. Cynder gave her a dirty look.

"I'm looking for my Aunt Krystal or Ed," Cynder told the teacher.

"She said she'd be out back in the garden, check there," the teacher told her.

"May I take Grant with me?" she asked. Cynder didn't want him around Basha if she was going to be mean to him.

Grant seemed to understand what Cynder was saying. He walked over to the sandbox and took a fistful of sand and put it in his pocket. This too, was behavior Cynder had never seen in him before. She giggled at him.

Cynder took Grant's hand and they walked out to the back garden. Grant gently touched the plants and flowers as they walked past them. Every once in a while he wanted to stop and look closer. Cynder sniffed some of the flowers and he copied her. Then she had an idea, she took her necklace off and put it around Grant's neck. *This might help him to heal*, she thought.

They were coming around a path to a garden as Krystal and Ed were coming out.

"Hey Cynder," Ed said smiling, "We were just talking about you."

"Oh yeah?" Cynder questioned suspiciously.

"Don't look so puzzled," Aunt Krystal said, "It was good things, like how much Grant has changed since you've been working with him. I'll take Grant back to his room, so you and Ed can go plant shopping."

Cynder bent down and took her necklace back from Grant. Aunt Krystal tried to take his hand, as Cynder had done, and he refused to give it to her.

Krystal smiled sweetly at Cynder. "I guess I don't have the magic like you do Cynder."

Odd choice of words, Cynder thought.

"Grant, go with Aunt Krystal," Cynder said. "He has a pocketful of sand," she told Krystal.

They all laughed.

"I like the students to call me Ms. Krystal."

"Oh, right, sorry." Cynder bent down and put her face to Grant's. "You need to go back with Ms. Krystal now."

He took Krystal's hand. "See what I mean?" Krystal said to Ed.

He nodded.

Cynder told Ed about the woman in the red car and how she spun the gravel.

"That woman is trouble Cynthia; you'd do best not to confront her."

When they got to the Landscapes of Eden, Cynder exited Ed's truck before it even quit coughing. Ed was a little slower and he laughed at her enthusiasm.

When Ed caught up to Cynder she was at the back of the house.

Ed approached a man in a nearby shed and talked for a few minutes. Then he walked over to Cynder. "Jake says we can pick out whatever we want and he can bill it to us."

Cynder hoped Jake was her father, but she wondered exactly how she was going to be able to tell. She was glad she was finally going to meet him so that she would know a little bit more.

"Is he going to come help us at all?" Cynder pushed.

"He'll be out momentarily Cynthia. It's not a problem; we can walk around all we want. We have all day ya know."

"Oh I know," she said excitedly.

She and Ed walked around discussing the flowering plants with their various colors and textures. He was quite impressed with her and really took to her, agreeing with all of her suggestions.

"Now to attract hummingbirds," Cynder said, "you'd want some trumpet honeysuckles, salvias, or a cigar plant. You'd also want to have some birdbaths around too. Everyone would enjoy watching them and bird watching is calming for autistics."

"Spoken from a true expert," sounded a deep voice from behind Cynder.

Cynder spun around on her heels almost knocking herself into the plants. She had to look almost straight up to see his face. He stood a good foot taller than her.

"You sure do know a lot, for a young girl. You must be Cynthia." He offered his hand as a way of introduction.

Cynder froze, she knew he was the 'J' she was looking for and she believed him to be her father. He was tall and handsome with dark blonde hair and warm green eyes. He was around the age of her mother, so that fit. His smile was kind and inviting.

"Hello," he said, causing Cynder to snap out of it.

"Hello," she greeted him kindly.

"I'm Jake, or you can call me 'J.' Lots of my close friends do," Jake said.

And there it was; verification that he was 'J.' Cynder wanted to throw her arms around him and call him father, but she resisted.

"Cynthia is our resident expert." Ed said, "I am told that she knows a lot about the world of gardening. We have entrusted a big job to her and we really need to start picking out plants for the Pleiades School."

"Oh, anything you want. I'll even give you a big discount because I believe in what they're doing out there," he touched his hand to his heart and tilted his head at Cynder. "This is a project close to my own heart."

Does he think I'm one of the autistic students, Cynder questioned herself?

"I'm a volunteer," Cynder informed him, her voice was shaky.

"I would love to volunteer too, if that's possible." He motioned towards Ed, "I could help you put the flowers in."

Cynder's heart sank. *My father wants to help me.*

"We do have a lot of heavy pots that need to be moved," said Ed, "and speaking for myself and Cynthia, it is some pretty heavy lifting that I'm sure we don't want to try to manage by ourselves."

Cynder shook her head yes.

"Excellent," Jake said, "let's get started by picking out some plants. We can go out back to the greenhouse to start."

Cynder was very nervous as they were walking through the rows of flowering plants. Jake suggested they view all of the plants before they made a selection. She had a million questions that she wanted to ask him, and none of them were about plants. Ed stopped to look at some flowers and was out of earshot, Cynder took the opportunity to ask Jake some questions.

"Are you moving?" she asked nervously.

He stopped and looked at her, tilting his head to one side and pursing his lips. "No. Why do you ask?"

"I stopped out here yesterday and there was a moving van here."

"That would have been my ex-wife. She moved away three years ago, and she came back into town to get some of her things."

"Are you married now?" The question uncontrollably popped out of Cynder's mouth.

"No and I don't have a lot of time for dating right now." He smiled, "I don't know why I'm telling you any of this."

"I'm sorry if I've asked too much." She wasn't really sorry though, she wanted to know everything about him.

"That's okay; you know I haven't talked too much to anyone about all of this."

Jake's phone began to ring. He excused himself from
Cynder and walked away. Cynder saw a flower with a broken
stem. She looked around to make sure that no one was
watching her. She removed her necklace from her neck and
knelt down. She held the stem in one hand and her lapis
stone in the other. She worked the way Lazuli had taught her
and the flower healed instantly.

Cynder was pleased that she could help the flower. She
had been practicing in her own garden and felt proud of how
well she could heal the flowers, plants, and more.

Time had flown by and it was lunch time. Jake invited
them to stay for lunch. Cynder thought she might be
uncomfortable, but she hoped this would give her more of an
opportunity to know Jake.

They sat out at a picnic table and Jake brought out
sandwiches and chips and sodas. Ed ate three sandwiches. It
took Cynder all of the control she had to keep from asking
Jake a lot of personal questions. Ed told a lot of funny stories
about his life when he was younger. Cynder enjoyed
conversations with both of them. They both acted like they
knew each other though. They had an enjoyable lunch.
Before they knew it two hours had gone by. They all decided
they needed to get back to work.

Jake, Cynder, and Ed picked out some flowers. Cynder
intentionally picked out only a few today, so that she would
have to come back. Jake helped them to load the truck and
said he would be out later in the week to help with some of
the planting.

C. Logan Anthony

CYNDER

CHAPTER THIRTEEN

On the ride back to the school Cynder was smiling wider than a daisy in full bloom. Ed told her how much he was impressed with her.

"Do you work for the Pleiades or are you a volunteer?" Cynder asked Ed.

Ed laughed. "I guess I could fit into both categories, but let's just say I'm volunteering."

"Do you have enough money for food?" Again, a question popped out of Cynder's mouth when she was just thinking it.

"Of course I do." He took his focus off the road and turned to her, "Now Cynthia, why would you ask me if I can buy food?"

"I'm sorry; it's just that you seemed so hungry at Jake's

and your clothes…they are uh… well…"

"Oh, my clothes don't look so nice? Well, you see Cynthia, I don't care what people think of my clothes," he said kindly. "I could wear suits that cost a thousand dollars every day if I wanted to, but then I would have to sit in my house or an office. How much fun would that be?"

"None, I suppose," Cynder said. She had never sat in an office and thought he probably never did either.

"When I dress in these comfortable clothes I get to do things like this. It has been a lot of fun today, wouldn't you agree?"

"Yes, a lot of fun," Cynder confessed. She began to feel bad for even saying anything. She pulled on her necklace. With her head hanging she thought about how painful it has been for her when the girls at school teased her about her clothes.

"I don't want people to like me for my clothes. I want to be liked for me," Ed said.

Cynder shook her head. She knew how he felt and she wanted to share her own experiences with him, "Ed, I get teased at school about my clothes. My mother even gives me a hard time."

Ed nodded his head but kept his gaze to the road.

"I'm sorry I said anything about your clothes or the food. I guess I did the same thing to you that people have done to me… um I assumed that because of the way that you dressed, that you were different, that you didn't have any money. I'm really sorry."

Ed nodded his head again.

She went on, "I don't have any friends; my mom bugs me about that too. I think the more I get teased about my clothes, especially by my mom, the more stubborn I get about them."

Ed said, "Only you know who you want to be and only you can make that happen. I, like you, want people to like me for me, not how I dress or what I can do for them."

"You mean like taking me out to the landscaping place?"

"That was something I wanted to do. Ever since I saw you with Grant, I knew you were special..."

Cynder's mind jumped to: *What did he see?*

"...that and the flowers," he continued, "I've never seen a young person that was so interested and talented with the flowers." He pulled into the school and turned to Cynder, "You keep being yourself Cynthia, and you'll have a strong future ahead of you."

When Cynder got back to the school she looked for Sheridan. She approached Grant's classroom and heard Krystal speaking firmly to someone in the room.

"You may not come into this school anytime you want. Ms. Black, I must ask you to leave at once."

Cynder turned to enter the room and was nearly bowled over by the woman as she charged out. Cynder thought she received an intentional push as the woman fled the room. The woman didn't seem to remember Cynder from the Landscapes of Eden, when she met her there a few days ago.

Cynder watched her storm down the hallway. The woman flung the door open as she exited the school, and the door banged against the door stop and flipped back.

Cynder went into the classroom. "Why was she here?" Cynder asked Aunt Krystal.

"That witch is Grant's mother," she spat. "But she's not supposed to be here. She doesn't have custody of Grant and I don't know if she has any visitation rights either." Krystal paused and took a deep breath and let it out. "She's been abusive to Grant; and has gone to jail for it. We need to keep her away." She shook her head and shoulders as though she were shrugging off a coat. "Sorry, I don't mean to get you involved, but if you ever see her here again, come find me or let Ed know."

"But who is she?"

"Eva…Eva Black. Like I said she's Grant's mother. Trouble, that's what she is," Krystal affirmed.

"Is she-"

Krystal cut her off abruptly, "I really need to go to the office and look into this. Cynder, what did you need?" she asked sharply. She put her hand on Cynder's shoulder; she took a deep breath and let it out again to calm herself. She spoke in a softer voice, "I'm sorry honey, what can I do for you?"

"I'm looking for Sheridan. He was giving me a ride home."

"Oh," Krystal said, "He and Basha were in the gym last I knew." Krystal turned sharply and scuttled out of the room.

"Basha," Cynder growled deep in her throat. She banged her fists against the sides of her legs. Why did they bother her so much?

Cynder was trying to think of another way to get home so that she wouldn't need to ride with them, when they walked around the corner.

"Hey Cynder," Sheridan said, "I was just telling Basha about your wonderful garden. I told her you were the best gardener I have ever known."

"I can't wait to see it," said Basha.

"Oh," said Cynder, "did he tell you that no one is allowed in my garden?" She threw Sheridan a dirty look. "It's private," she enunciated the words. "It can be scary there. Did Sheridan tell you how he fell on his butt one day? Something grabbed him and it really spooked him. He left that garden so fast, ha ha." Cynder glanced at Sheridan when she laughed. "I didn't think he would ever come back." Cynder walked over close to Basha, she leaned in towards her, she whispered, "There is something there…I've seen things…"

Basha's eyes got big as Cynder held her gaze.

Sheridan paused for a moment. He said, "Aw Cynder. Who knows what it was. Anyway, let's get going."

As they walked out of the school, Cynder saw Ed across the parking lot getting into his truck. "I'm riding with Ed out to the landscaping place. I'll see you tomorrow Sheridan."

She hurried off before Sheridan had time to question her.

CHAPTER FOURTEEN

On their way out to Landscapes from Eden, Ed asked Cynder how she was enjoying her volunteer job at the school.

"I like it," she said, "at first I thought I was just going be doing gardening, but now I'm really enjoying the kids, especially the young ones."

"Yes I've noticed you a lot with Grant, the little one; he really likes you, and you have taken to him real well. I see you pay a lot of attention to him, but not the other kids, but I guess that's okay. He really has changed a lot since you've been around." He got a far off look on his face, "It's like he is becoming normal."

Cynder nodded her head.

"Why do you want to go back out to the Landscapes of Eden?"

Cynder hadn't thought ahead of time how she was going to answer that question, so the truth popped out, as the truth usually does, especially when you have no lie prepared. "I just didn't want to ride with Sheridan and Basha." She looked down at her necklace and began to play with it.

"I did notice Sheridan has an eye for her. Is he supposed to be yours?" Ed asked gently.

"Oh no, no, not at all," Cynder said emphatically, "it's just that we've been best friends since I was little. In fact, he's the only friend I've had since I was little." Cynder turned her head and looked out her window.

"And if the shoe were on the other foot?" Ed asked.

"What you mean?" Cynder turned back to look at Ed.

"What if you liked somebody in that way?"

"I don't." She said it like she had been fed a spoonful of medicine.

"You will someday." Ed argued.

"No I don't think so." Cynder scrunched her face up.

"I'm going in with you and to make sure that Jake is here. And you know what? I think I'll just stick around for a while and pick out a plant for my wife."

"You're married?" Cynder said, surprised.

"Think my clothes are too ratty to get a woman huh?" Ed teased. "I have a fine wife."

"Well no… I just… Well, I…" Cynder looked down at her hands, trying to figure out how she was going to get herself out of this one.

"I'm just picking on you, little one." Ed laughed as he pulled into the drive of Jake's place.

Cynder looked up and saw Jake walking into the greenhouse. She jumped out of the truck before it came to a complete stop. She was all the way to the greenhouse by the time Ed even made it up to the house.

"Jake, hey Jake," Cynder called, as she ran towards him.

"Cynthia, glad to see you," Jake called back. He stopped what he was doing to greet her.

"What brings you here so late in the day, not changing your mind on that order are you?" Jake asked as he walked towards her.

"Oh no, it's not that at all." Again, Cynder had not thought this out ahead of time. What excuse was she going to use for going out there? Ed didn't push her for an explanation, and she was glad about that. Sheridan didn't ask her and she was glad about that too. Before she could even think of anything Jake started talking.

"I have a plant that I'd like you to take a look at," Jake pointed outside, "it has a variety of rich green colors that will accent a lot of the flowers that you're putting in. Hosta plants are blue herbaceous perennials. The most natural way to group them is by leaf-color. The foliage can be blue, yellow, or green. Or sometimes, one will find a pleasing blend, as when there's just enough yellow and green to form chartreuse. In addition to all this variety in color, the foliage is immaculate. Not only do they look beautiful Cynthia, but the fragrance is…"

Cynder was only half listening to what he was saying. Before Ed came over to them, she wanted to get right to the question that she was so curious about. She wanted to know if he was still hooked up with this woman Eva.

"Jake I've been wondering –" but before she could even get her question out, of all things, something slammed into the side of her leg.

"Cinderella, Cinderella," Grant chanted clinging to her leg.

Cynder knelt down to him, and placed one hand on his shoulder and the other hand on his head. "Grant what are you doing here?"

Of course, Grant didn't answer her question. He looked up at Jake. Then Cynder looked up at Jake and saw that Jake's mouth was hanging wide open.

There was silence between them and Cynder looked back down at Grant. After a long pause, Cynder looked back up to Jake.

"Cinderella, you see me?" Grant said hugging Cynder's leg.

"Yes, I see you Grant."

Jake fell to his knees and knelt next to Grant. "Grant... Grant what did you say?" Jake pulled Grant gently from Cynder's leg and held him in his arms. "How do you know... of course you know Grant, you work at the school. He talks to you? He never talks to anyone." Tears streamed down Jake's face. "And I'm usually the only one that can ever touch him. He barely let his own mother touch him."

"You mean Eva... So Eva... Eva is your wife?"

"Eva is my ex-wife. She said she came back to get some of her things from the house. But trouble follows that woman... dangerous trouble."

"I saw her at the school today," Cynder reported.

"Yes, Miss Krystal called me and told me she was there. Grant is scared half to death of her, and he usually runs in the other direction when he sees her." Jake looked lovingly down at Grant, "I can't believe he has taken to you so well in such a short time and I think it's great." He smiled at Cynder, "I think you're great, I can't think of a better person to be around him."

Cynder smiled back at him, she could feel tears welling up in her eyes. It occurred to her, that if Jake was her father, then Grant must be her brother. No wonder they had a special connection.

Cynder bent down to them and gave them a quick hug, she wasn't ready to tell Jake who she was, and more importantly she wasn't ready to ask him if he was her father.

"Oh, there you are," Ed yelled from about twenty five yards away, "I found a plant for my wife. Did you find what you are looking for Cynthia?"

"I think I found everything that I am looking for," Cynder said, holding back her tears.

CHAPTER FIFTEEN

Ed dropped Cynder off at home. She headed straight for her garden; she wanted to talk to Gilly. She was so happy and so excited she had to share with someone. She didn't know quite how to contain herself. She skipped straight to the gate of the garden. She swung the gate open and was shocked to find Sheridan and Basha sitting on the bench locked in a kiss. She froze where she was standing, not sure what to do. After a long moment she stepped in and slammed the gate shut. This halted the kiss instantly, and they both sprang off the bench.

"Cynder," Sheridan quavered, "I was just… We were just…" His face flushed and he looked down at his feet, he shoved both of his hands into his pockets. Basha stepped behind him and hung her head; her brown hair fell across her face like the close of a curtain.

"I know what you were just doing," Cynder snarled, "I am fourteen you know." She walked past them scowling as she headed towards her Gaillardia flowers. "I'd like some privacy in my sanctuary, if you two don't mind," she grumbled, "and Sheridan, I will talk to you later."

Sheridan and Basha exchanged glances, and headed towards the gate. They didn't have to be asked twice, they ran out of Cynder's garden as fast as they could.

Cynder hadn't been to the back of the garden for a long time. The only flowers were wild flowers and they didn't need her care. There were many trees and plants and Cynder thought it was beautiful, peaceful. She found a big oak tree at the back of the garden and climbed it as high as she could go. She walked out on a limb, turned and looked down. It was a long way down. Below her were large rocks, a small creek, and a pool of water.

"No one would even care if I jumped out of this tree and died," Cynder said calmly. She had no intention of jumping, but she was frustrated and couldn't understand why so many things were upsetting her.

"I would care," Gilly whispered.

"Thanks, I knew you would," Cynder told Gilly, relieved that she showed up.

Gilly flew to the branch and climbed out on a leaf and sat down. She looked down at the wild flowers in the garden where lots of butterflies flew on the gentle breeze.

"That was 'the Basha' with Sheridan wasn't it? I saw them. Can you believe it? He had the nerve to bring 'the Basha' here when you made it quite clear that you didn't want her here."

"Yeah, I know," Cynder grunted. "But I need to talk to you about something else now."

Gilly propped her elbows on her knees and settled her chin on her fists, and gave Cynder her full attention.

"I went out to Jake's after school," Cynder said, tears began to pour out with her words. "Grant is his son, and Eva is his ex-wife. If he's my father, that means Grant is my brother. Do you know what this means? This means I have a brother." She smiled through her tears.

"This is great?" Gilly partly questioned and partly agreed. She couldn't tell if Cynder was crying happy tears or sad tears. "When are you going to tell Jake?"

"I haven't figured that out yet. When should I tell him? Tell me how it is going to come out when I tell him. Will he be happy about it?"

"If you're waiting for me to tell you, I can't. I don't know."

"No really, just tell me and then it won't be so hard to figure out when to tell him."

"You know I can't tell you anything. I don't want to get into trouble, or lose the garden. And I like to watch you in your dreams and how you're working with Grant. I want to stick around and see what else happens."

"I thought you knew what was going to happen…like a psychic."

"Ha ha," Gilly laughed hard, holding her stomach, and doing backward somersaults in the air.

"What's so funny about that?" Cynder said, greatly insulted.

Gilly flew in front of Cynder. "You believe in psychics." Gilly teased.

"Why shouldn't I? It's no different than believing in fairies," Cynder grunted. "My mother believes in psychics. She says they're real."

"I am real obviously," Gilly announced as she held her hands out as if modeling her outfit. "But psychics, really, plus they're human."

"Let's get back to my original question. Why won't you tell me anything about my father? Why doesn't my mother talk about him?"

"I do know that if you try to talk to her she will give you the answers you seek. It may take a few times trying. That's all I can say."

"Do you know your father Gilly?"

A strange look came over Gilly's face. "You know, I never thought about that before. I don't think I have a father in the way humans do, I have a creator."

"Oh," said Cynder. "It didn't really bother me so much that I didn't have a father either, until I found that letter. It was written when I was younger, I know it. It bothers me that I could have had a father all of this time and my mother didn't let me know him." Cynder looked down. She had tears streaming down her face.

"I know it's difficult for you Cynder," but keep pursuing it, you will find what you are looking for. You will find where you belong."

Cynder turned to look at Gilly, but she was gone. Then she heard an explosion, like a firecracker. She knew this was Gilly's exit.

Cynder climbed out of the tree and went to the small pool of water. She sat on a large rock in the middle of the pool and took her shoes off and placed her feet in the cool water.

She watched the pool of water twirling softly around her feet. She felt relieved and completely relaxed. It felt, to her, like the water was taking her troubles away. She put her hands down in the water and the dirt was cleansed from them.

The wind began to pick up and the trees and plants around her began to rock gently back and forth. Cynder noticed that the wind was swirling only around the pool. She heard, what she thought was a woman whispering, but she couldn't make out whose voice it was or what it was saying.

"Gilly, are you trying to trick me?" She sat and listened for her, but no Gilly. "Lazuli are you there?" No Lazuli.

Then the voice started to speak words that Cynder could understand. They said, "Go to the cottage now Cynder."

Most people would be scared of this, but it didn't scare Cynder. She thought it was calming. She felt safe with the voice and decided to talk to it.

"Okay, I will go home." She waited but heard no more.

Cynder skipped to the house and found her mother at the stove cooking dinner. Cynder rushed to her, and threw her arms around her. "I love you mom," Cynder whispered and backed away from her.

"What?" Jessilyn asked, she was shocked by Cynder's display. She slowly turned around.

"I'm going to change before dinner." Cynder hurried out of the room.

Cynder put on one of her new white dresses. She brushed her hair up into a ponytail, and joined her mother in the kitchen.

"Well this is refreshing," Jessilyn said as Cynder walked into the room.

When they sat down to eat Cynder clasped her lapis stone in her fingers and began to fiddle with it. She was nervous; she wanted to get her mom talking about personal things and didn't quite know where to start. She hadn't talked to her mom like this, ever. She bit her bottom lip.

"Mom, I want to ask you something," Cynder said, "did you date when you were in high school?"

"I should have known you were up to something." Jessilyn slapped her fork on the table.

"No Mom," Cynder pleaded, "it's not what you think." Cynder reached over and patted her mother's hand, picked her fork up, and placed it gently back into her hand.

Jessilyn was surprised. This was a side of Cynder that she had never seen before. Her face softened. "What is it then?" she said reluctantly.

"Sheridan likes this girl that's volunteering at the school. Her name is Basha," Cynder waved her hand in the air, to show her contempt for the name and the person.

"That's nice," Jessilyn said, "he has a little friend. Basha. That is an odd name." Her mind drifted off. She took a deep breath and looked back at Cynder blankly; she shook her head and sighed, "Anyways..." Jessilyn flipped her hand and focused back on Cynder.

"No Mom, it's not nice. I mean it is probably nice for him, but I feel kind of funny about it and I can't figure out why. It's not like I like him in that way," Cynder said, placing her palm to her chest.

"Tell me a little bit about Basha."

"She looks kind of plain. Not pretty. Long brown hair. She's nothing special. She's shorter than me." Cynder paused, trying to think of something bad to say about her. "I've seen her doing mean things to the autistic children. Not anything big, but mean little things." Cynder paused, waiting for her mother's reaction.

"Are you jealous of her?"

"No of course not…" Cynder didn't think so. She took a moment to think. She tilted her head to the side. "Probably a little," Cynder admitted shrugging her shoulders. "But it's like… like I don't understand how I'm feeling all of a sudden. I get upset and I don't know why."

"Cynder," Jessilyn said, "all girls, as they become women, go though confusing times like this. It's caused by the body changing and growing up." Her mother leaned in and whispered, "Hormones." She nodded her head. "It will pass Cynder, I promise."

"But what about boys, Mom," Cynder said. She was fishing, trying to get her mother to talk about her own experiences when she was young. "When will I understand boys?"

Jessilyn laughed softly, "Never." She turned and gazed at the bouquet of flowers in the center of the table. "I remember my first love…my high school sweetheart." She paused for a moment. "Actually he is the only one I've ever loved…"

Cynder remained quiet hoping that it was Jake that she was talking about. Her mother had never talked guys or about being in love.

Tears welled up in Jessilyn's eyes, she shifted in her chair. She looked back at Cynder. "He was your…" her chin quivered, "he is your father."

Cynder felt uncomfortable. She almost wished she wouldn't have started this conversation when she saw how sad it made her mother. She held her breath and brought her napkin to her face to conceal her own emotion, excitement mixed with dread, in case she wasn't talking about Jake. Cynder wanted to know why she has kept him from her all these years. *What if Jake isn't my father, do I want to hear this?*

"It was a high school crush, my mother called it," Jessilyn said staring at her plate of food, her mouth pouting as she spoke. "It couldn't be serious mother vowed."

Her mother looked so sad Cynder could barely go on. But she had started this painful conversation and she needed to know.

"What happened?" Cynder said in a faint voice, her eyes welling up with tears. She bit her lip to keep her chin from quivering.

"Too much to go into right now, Cynder." Jessilyn said sadly, wiping the tears from the corners of her eyes with her napkin.

"But Mom," Cynder pleaded, "I have a right to know. Please tell me."

"All I will tell you right now is that my mother interfered and so did another girl. It wasn't going to work out." Jessilyn's chin quivered again. By now her mascara turned her tears to mud and they ran down her face. She began to shovel her food into her mouth. "I have told you plenty for now and that's all there is to it."

Cynder could hardly bear to see her mother in pain, with her face smudged black. She looked like a toddler that had gotten out of control with a marker. She was so sad, so upset, so pained…

Her mother had told all she was going to tell tonight.

CHAPTER SIXTEEN

The next day Jake delivered the plants to the school. He jumped out of his truck grinning handsomely, when he waved to Cynder.

Cynder ran to the truck. She had been looking forward to this day.

"I brought you a present," Jake announced. He thrust a box into Cynder's hands.

"What?" Cynder asked, confused. "Why did you get me a present?"

"Every good gardener needs these. Open it." He seemed excited to be giving.

Cynder threw the top off the box to reveal a green and blue gardener's apron and matching gloves. The apron was printed with wild flowers and had two big pockets in the front.

Jake said, "You can't mess up that pretty white dress and we have a lot of work to do today. Try it on."

"Thank you," Cynder squealed. She tied the apron on and glided her hands into the gloves.

"That color looks great on you, I thought it would," Jake told her.

"I would hate to get this dirty." Cynder said. She ran her hands down the front of the apron.

"Don't worry about that," Jake said, "it can be washed over and over again."

Cynder never left Jake's side that day. Ed came and went as they were working on projects, and Cynder showed Jake that she wasn't afraid to work hard. They planted trees and flowers in front of the school and potted several plants to decorate the inside of the school.

They talked and laughed and he was so nice to Cynder, she couldn't believe it.

Before Cynder knew it, the end of the school day had come. Cynder didn't want the day to be over.

Jake invited Cynder to come over on Saturday to see his pottery studio. He told her to get permission from her mother. Of course, Cynder could not ask her mother, what would she say? She knew her mother worked all day on Saturday, so she planned on riding her bike there.

Every minute dragged until Saturday morning came. Cynder packed her backpack with her new apron and gloves, and a bottle of water for the long bicycling stretch ahead of her to Jake's place.

Cynder had been thinking for days about how to get him to talk about cremation urns. She knew he had made the one for her grandmother, and she wanted him to tell her about it. She was eager to learn a little bit about her grandmother and hoping that this would lead to him talking about her mother too.

Jake and Grant were excited to see Cynder, and Grant ran out chanting 'Cinderella.' Jake's pottery studio was in the large lean-to on the back of the house.

Cynder pulled her apron out of her backpack but Jake stopped her. "Oh no, you don't want to use this apron," Jake said, "It will get stained. I have other aprons you can use." He went to the wall where several aprons hung. He chose a clean one, and handed it to Cynder. These aprons were very different than her gardening apron, they didn't have any pockets, and they were a dull white. The one he handed her was clean, but was stained orange and brown in places from previous use around the clay. Grant had a small apron on too.

Jake described his love of pottery. He put a ball of clay in the center of a round disk on top of a contraption that he called a pottery wheel. He flipped on a switch and began to spin the wheel by pushing on a pedal with his foot. He dipped his hand into a bowl of water and explained the process to Cynder as he was working. He stuck his wet thumb down in the center of the ball of clay. Cynder was surprised at how quickly the shape began to turn into a bowl.

He told Cynder that he would do one first to show her how and then it would be her turn. She looked around the shop and saw a few new cremation urns that looked similar to her grandmother's, sitting on the shelves.

"Boy," Cynder said, "I bet you could really tell some stories about cremation urns."

"Yeah, I have lots of stories," Jake said, not taking his eyes off the project he was working on. "Not many people have heard about my cremation urns. Some people find it down-right creepy, but I think it's a good idea."

Cynder looked over at Grant; he had his own little table with a turntable on it. It was obvious he was trying to mimic what Jake was doing.

Jake looked over at him too. "Grant's trying to use clay like I do, that's a new thing that he started a few days ago. I never thought he was paying attention to me before."

Cynder knew exactly why Grant's behavior was changing.

Cynder felt she had to be more creative with her questions to get Jake to tell cremation urn stories. She was wracking her brain to try to come up with a question that would not give away that she knew very much.

"What made you start making cremation urns?" Cynder

asked.

"My mom and I used to make bowls, jars, pots for plants, and things like that, but when she got sick I wanted to do something special for her before she died," Jake said. He pulled his hands away from the project, parked them on his thighs, and sat back on his stool and looked at Cynder. "She was real sick, so I wanted to make something just for her that wasn't like anything anybody else ever had. She is the one that taught me how to make pottery." He pointed down at his wheel. "In fact, this one was hers. She loved owls, so after I made the urn I made neat little owls to put all over it. When I took it to her I told her it was just a flower vase, and I put fresh flowers in it next to her bed every day. She loved it," he said, smiling as he returned his attention to the wheel.

Cynder couldn't believe the love that showed in his eyes when he was talking tenderly about his mother. He had a sad smile on his face when he talked about her though. Cynder thought that it was wonderful that he did something like this for his mother.

"Did you make any other ones for older women?" Cynder asked, probing him.

"I've made plenty of them for older women," he said, concentrating on his project. "A lot of women like me to embed their old jewelry into the urn before the clay dries."

There was a long silence. Cynder needed to come up with more pointed questions.

"I love fairies," Cynder said, "have you ever put fairies on any?"

"As a matter of fact I have." Jake said. He didn't elaborate.

"Any story on that one?" Cynder ventured. He wasn't playing into her questions like she wanted him to. A long pause passed and Cynder could think of nothing else to get him to go further.

Then he surprised her.

"Well…" Jake said. He looked up from his work again and rubbed the back of his neck. "I had this one lady that came to me, and I was quite surprised that she did, because she never really liked me."

Cynder slipped onto a stool next to him and nodded her head, urging him to go on.

"This woman had brain cancer and she was dying from it. She didn't have very long to live. She claimed to talk to fairies in her garden, but I wasn't sure that her illness wasn't making her lose her mind a little bit. She said the fairies tried to heal her, but it was too late." Jake smiled softly and put his hands back on the clay. "She said the fairies helped her to heal her heart, but they couldn't help her with her brain."

They exchanged glances and smiled. Now Cynder knew that her grandmother saw fairies in the garden too. *If he only knew that fairies can help heal,* Cynder thought, *and this is why Grant is getting better.*

"She said that being faced with death made her realize some things that she had handled wrong in life, and that holding onto grudges, like she had been, was doing nothing to help her. She said she lost her daughter and granddaughter because of her anger. She took responsibility for the fact that her daughter didn't have a husband and that her granddaughter was growing up without a father or any grandparents."

Jake shook his head and tears came to his eyes. He switched off the motor of the wheel and went to the sink to rinse his hands. His quaking shoulders almost made Cynder run out of the studio. She felt awkward, uncomfortable. He sobbed silently and took a long time to rinse his hands. He filled his hands with water and plunged his face into them.

Cynder took her apron and wiped her own face that had become soaked. For some reason these tears stung worse than any other tears ever did. She remained silent.

Jake pulled a towel from the rack and wiped off his hands and his face. He took a deep breath and turned around letting it out. "Yeah, she thought that all of her anger was probably what made her sick."

"Oh," Cynder said softly. She was also beginning to understand why her mother was so bitter.

Jake shrugged his shoulders and leaned against the workbench. "I think she came to me more to apologize than to have me make her an urn."

"Apologize-," Cynder said, "for what?"

"Like I said, she never really liked me, so the fact that I liked her daughter in high school didn't go over too well with her."

"Oh," Cynder said. This was what her mother was trying to tell her, but it was too painful for her. Now Cynder knew why.

"But you know what Cynder? It wasn't really me that she didn't like; she had never liked my mother way back from when they were in high school. Silly thing isn't it?" Jake said. He tossed his towel on the workbench.

"Why didn't she like your mother?" Cynder inquired. She hoped it wasn't something real serious.

"She said that my mother stole her boyfriend when they were in high school, and that boyfriend was my dad." He tilted his head towards Cynder and shook his head back and forth.

"Oh," said Cynder, "and she held a grudge all those years?"

"You had to know this woman. She held grudges, and she was angry most of her life. Mean… boy that woman was mean. She was so angry with what life had handed her. It's a shame, a crying shame, that people can be this way. She took it out on her daughter so badly that she drove her away right after she graduated from high school. Her daughter went away for college and never moved back home."

"Why was she so angry with her daughter?"

"Well you see Cynder, her daughter and I dated all through high school. Her mom was always trying to break us up, just because she didn't like my mother. And well…we snuck behind her back one summer when her daughter came home from college and we spent the whole summer seeing each other. Her daughter lied to her all summer. It was the wrong way to go about it, I realize that now. But we were in love; it wasn't just a high school crush like she said. We wanted to get married someday. We didn't know what else to do."

"Why didn't you get married anyway?"

"I asked her, but she wouldn't come back. She said she wanted to finish college. She felt like she couldn't talk to her mother about anything."

"Oh, that's so sad." This reminded Cynder of what she says about her own mother.

"We got into a huge argument about it and we drifted apart. I waited for her to graduate. She said to give her two years, but then she never came back. I know that her mother told her about Eva. She never liked Eva. I had no way of getting a hold of her and her mother wouldn't tell me anything."

"And now?" Cynder asked.

"And now what?" Jake looked at her confused and tilted his head to the side.

"Well, do you still love her?" Cynder pleaded to him with her eyes to please say 'yes he still loved her mother.'

"I do… yes I do, Cynthia. But so much has changed now." He shook his head and looked over at Grant. "I have Grant, and she's moved away. I can't take Grant away, especially now that the special school has opened. I'm not even sure where she is." He rubbed the back of his neck and shook his head. "Her mother took so much from me it nearly killed me." He started to cry again. "But I forgave her…I had to forgive her, and the love of my life is gone." He wiped his tears on the back of his hand and picked up the towel again. "I'm sorry to put all of this on you Cynthia; you're just so easy to talk to." He sniffled.

Cynder screamed in her head, *The love of your life is right here in this town, and your daughter is standing right in front of you.* Cynder was about to cry. She needed to leave before the tears spilled out. She resorted to lying.

"Oh, it's getting late and I told my mother I'd be home by now. I've got to go." She ran to Jake and gave him a quick hug, tore off her apron, and returned it to the hook. She ran over and tousled Grant's hair. "Bye Grant. Jake, can I come back tomorrow?"

"Of course, Cynder, you are welcome here any time."

CHAPTER SEVENTEEN

Cynder woke up Sunday morning and told her mother she was going for a bike ride. When her mother pressed her for where she was going, she lied again, and said that she wanted the exercise and that she wanted to check out some flowers she had seen growing along a corn field. Her mother instructed her to be home in two hours because they were scheduled to have dinner at Krystal's house.

Cynder rode as fast as she could to Jake's house. It took her almost half an hour to get to his place. She knew she only had one hour to spend with him today.

When she pedaled up to his house she was out of breath. Grant almost knocked her down when he ran to her and hugged her.

"I think it's neat how much Grant likes you. I've never seen him take to anyone like he takes to you. And I've never heard him so verbal with anyone before. Where does he get this Cinderella stuff from anyways?"

"I don't know," Cynder lied. She couldn't tell him it was from a dream. And then she began to wonder, *How is it that it was my dream, yet Grant remembers it?* This was most certainly a question to ask Gilly or Lazuli, but she had the feeling that energy would have something to do with it.

"I have a lot of plants to pot today Cynder, if you want to help me. The local woman's club is coming out here on Monday and I need to get these done." He scratched the back of his neck, "Let's see I have five done and I need twenty more. Are you up to it?"

"Sure," Cynder said, pulling her new apron out of her back pack. "Where do we start?"

"I can bring the pots from the pottery studio, and here are the bags of dirt, with a trowel." He pointed across the yard. "I've got the plants out in front of the greenhouse, if you want to bring them over. There are Shasta Daisies there, some Pansies, red Gerbera, orange Gerbera, Begonia, and my favorite, Ice Blue Clematis. In fact why don't you take one of those plants home with you. I can rig a basket to your bike."

"Okay," said Cynder, and she headed for the greenhouse. She turned back around to yell to Jake, "Oh, I only have an hour."

"Are you sure you want to work then?" Jake asked.

"Of course," Cynder said. She was as happy as could be working with flowers and her father.

Cynder worked as quickly as she could on the plants. She had fifteen of them potted when Jake brought another batch of pots to her.

"Whew," Jake said, "these pots are heavy. Wow, I can't believe you got so many of them finished. He looked at his watch. You've been here one hour and ten minutes. You should get going; I wouldn't want your mother mad at me."

"Do you know my mother?" Cynder asked. She didn't know why she asked it. The question just popped out of her mouth.

"No I don't think so," Jake said. "I probably should meet her sometime with you spending all this time here."

"You should meet her, you'd love her." Cynder said and she climbed onto her bike.

"Oh, wait a minute, let me get that basket for you," Jake said.

He hooked the basket onto Cynder's bike and put a pot of ice blue Clematis into it. "This is to thank you. Cynder, you sure are a good worker. There aren't many young kids like you."

Cynder got on her bike and rode down the driveway. She couldn't believe how happy she felt. She couldn't remember a time when she felt so happy.

"Next time, bring your mother over," Jake hollered.

"Sure," Cynder hollered back, "when she has time."

Cynder pedaled home as fast as she could, which was pretty easy to do because she was so excited about how her day had gone. When she got in the driveway her mother was waiting for her. She saw the potted flowers on Cynder's bike.

"You saw these flowers by the side of the road?" Jessilyn asked Cynder.

"Well, I... Well, I," Cynder stuttered.

"I can't believe you found these by the side of the road. You are so lucky. Did you know these are my favorite flowers?"

What an odd coincidence, Cynder thought, *that her mother and Jake would have the same favorite flower.*

"So, are you going to put them in your garden right away, or can we enjoy him in the house for a little while?" Jessilyn asked, "After all, they're already potted."

"Tell you what mom," Cynder said, "I got them for you." She thrust them into her mother's hands. Cynder thought to herself, *I have lied more this month than I have ever lied in my life.* But, she was really glad that her mother enjoyed them. Cynder never realized how happy her mother would get over a pot of flowers.

"Why, thank you, Cynder," she said, and she threw her arms around Cynder and gave her a long hug. "How did you keep your dress from getting dirty when you dug these up? And your hands, your hands are clean."

Cynder pulled her apron and gloves out of her backpack. "Because mom, I used these."

"Why didn't I ever think of that?" her mother said, shaking her head.

Cynder had a little bit of time to go into the garden before they had to leave for dinner. She needed to talk to a fairy, any fairy.

Lazuli came to her and Cynder asked about her grandmother.

Lazuli said, "With your grandmother it was too late to heal her physical body, but not too late to heal her heart. She needed to learn to get her thoughts away from her own desires, such as hate, anger, and resentment, and onto other's needs. The way you have with Grant."

"I haven't done that much for him," Cynder professed.

"But you have and you will do further work with him and with others. Look at how your world has expanded Cynder," Lazuli said. A rich color shimmered around her. "You have been helping at the school and with Grant. You have had the opportunity to do much of the gardening at the Pleiades School, and you have gotten closer to your mother. And even though you don't think of it this way, you have gotten to know your grandmother."

"Yeah," said Cynder flatly, "I don't think of my

grandmother that way."

"You see my dear, her heart was closed, and she wasn't ready to be with you." Lazuli put her hand on her own heart, "She had a cold heart Cynder, and she would have confused you more if you'd known her well. She would not have been a good teacher for you. She would have caused many difficulties for your mother."

"So, she was really that bad?"

"Her resentments, hate, and bitterness caused her illness. She also harmed the relationship she had with your mother and you in the process. She chose to be unhappy. We have a choice in life Cynder; we can choose to be happy if we want to be."

"And she was not happy," Cynder said deflated, "and my mother is not happy."

"Your grandmother was not meant to be with you at this time in your life." Lazuli said, "It is very difficult to explain something like this to a human so that you will understand it. She is with you, but not on this earth. She is with you in your heart and your mind. She left those pictures and letters for you."

"She knew I was going to find them?" asked Cynder.

"Let me say she was hoping that you would. It's all part of the magic, the way love works. Love can connect us over great distances and through time and it is energy, so it never dies."

Before dinner at Krystal's, Cynder approached Sheridan in his bedroom. This would be the first time they had talked since she found him and 'the Basha' kissing in her garden.

He had his back to the door and was playing a game on his computer.

Cynder walked in with a smug look on her face and plopped on the end of his bed. "You and 'the Basha' in my garden," she said, "now just how did that happen, Sheridan?"

He was startled at first, and then he turned around. "I know- I know Cynder, you told me not to take her there, but…" He looked down at his feet.

"But what Sheridan? She forced you; she cast some magic spell over you and tricked you into going there?"

His face blushed and he looked up. "You know, that's how it felt, Cynder."

"I don't buy that," Cynder said, and she rose from the end of the bed. "I know how you can make it up to me," she said smartly.

"How?" Sheridan asked reluctance in his voice.

"I want to ride shot-gun for the rest of the summer," she decided and nodded her head. She paused for no more than a second before she turned and walked out of the room.

At the dinner table the conversation came around to Cynder starting high school in the fall.

Krystal said, "Sheridan can show you around Cynder, but remember he has his own life there too." She gave a sideways glance to Jessilyn. "You need to look at this as an opportunity to make new friends."

Sheridan kept his head down, focusing on his plate; his tan face had gone pale.

Cynder felt like she'd been ambushed, this dinner was about Basha, and making sure that Cynder didn't get in the way of Sheridan and his 'other' interests. She felt her anger building up. She felt like her mom set her up.

She turned to her mother. "Mom, did you have friends in high school?"

Jessilyn was surprised; she didn't realize the conversation would turn to her. "I had a few friends, yes."

"Any of them boys?" Cynder pushed.

"Yes," Jessilyn blushed; she took a deep breath, and looked at Krystal and threw her a 'save me' look with her eyes.

"And whatever happened to that boy?" Cynder demanded to know.

"Well," said Jessilyn, sharply, she threw her shoulders back and slapped her fork on the table. "If you must know Cynder, my arch enemy from high school stole him when I was away at college."

Cynder didn't expect that answer and was at a loss for words. She must be talking about Eva Black. She needed to find her mother's high school yearbook to see if Eva went to school with them.

Jessilyn's face had become as red as a bright red regal Geranium. She looked down at her fork on the table.

Cynder looked at Sheridan, Krystal and his father, Sam. Their eyes pleaded with her to let it be.

The table became silent for a while.

Cynder slowly picked up her fork and began to push the food around on her plate. The others followed her lead.

Aunt Krystal broke the silence and changed the subject. "So Cynder I love what you're doing with the plants all around the Pleiades, you're so talented."

"Thank you Aunt Krystal," Cynder said.

CYNDER

CHAPTER EIGHTEEN

Cynder wanted to rush Monday away at the Pleiades so that she could hurry home and look in the Magic Box for her mother's year book. If she didn't find it there she would have to resort to the attic.

She had a lot of time to think about how her grandmother had resented an old high school rival and it ruined her life and made her unhappy. And now she knew that her mother was following the same pattern. Cynder decided she would break the pattern; otherwise she would be miserable for the rest of her life. She would forgive Sheridan for having Basha in her garden, and she would try to make friends with Basha at the school.

In the afternoon, Cynder took the fairy statue that looked like her to Grant, because of the three day weekend coming up she wanted him to take it home to help him feel secure. When Grant saw it he put it on top of a sand castle.

Cynder cringed. She really didn't want sand all over her fairy, but it was for Grant, so she didn't worry about it.

Basha and Sheridan walked into the room. They both cowered when they saw Cynder. "Hi guys," Cynder said with a pleasant voice. She waved them over to her table. "Sit down please."

Sheridan and Basha walked over by her and stood for a moment, she motioned for them to sit down.

"So, Basha," Cynder said with a kind voice, "what brings you to volunteer at the school?"

"I thought it would be good experience for me," she said in a soft voice.

"Oh, do you want to be a teacher?"

Basha shook her head no.

It surprised everyone in the room when Grant screamed, "Evil, evil." He grabbed the fairy statue from the sand castle with one hand and hit the side of his head with the other. "Ah ah," he was yelling and ran into the bathroom and slammed the door.

Cynder looked in the direction he was looking when he started screaming and she saw Eva standing in the doorway of the classroom.

The young teacher in the room shouted to Sheridan, "Go get Ms. Krystal, now please." He fled the room.

"Cynder, tend to Grant," the teacher said.

"Cynder?" Eva said stepping towards Cynder. "Your name is Cynder?"

"Yes," Cynder answered. She stood between Eva and the bathroom to protect Grant.

"That isn't a common name," Eva said, "who is your mother?"

"Jessilyn," Cynder answered. "Why?"

"Why? I'm sure you know why." Eva stepped closer to Cynder. "You ruined my life, you little brat."

Just then Krystal rushed into the room with Sheridan trailing behind her.

"Get away from her," Krystal said. She roared like a momma bear protecting her baby. She raced over to Eva and turned her around the way a person would flip a domino. "I have called the police and they are on their way. I suggest you leave before they get here if you want to avoid another arrest." Krystal got right up in her face.

Krystal stood a foot taller than Eva and was built bigger than her. Cynder thought, *If this turns into a fight, I know Aunt Krystal will take her.*

Eva backed down, but snarled at everyone. "You can't keep me from my son. I will be back," she vowed. "I hate you Cynder," she wailed. She stormed out. Everyone in the room could hear her heels slapping on the floor and she fled down the hallway.

Krystal processed the event with everyone. Cynder finally

got Grant to come out of the bathroom, but he clung to her leg while they waited for the bus.

Cynder made small talk with Sheridan and Basha until it was time to go home. The three of them walked to the car. Sheridan unlocked the door with a beep and he and Basha stopped a few feet before they got to the car.

"Hey Basha, you can have shot-gun," Cynder said, giving Sheridan a quick smile and she walked to the back door of the car.

Sheridan and Basha smiled at each other and at the same time, thanked Cynder.

When Cynder got home she looked in the magic box, hoping to find her mother's high school yearbook. She was careful and she pulled the contents from the box, remembering the order of everything. She had never been all the way to the bottom of the box before. Most of the things at the bottom of the box were useless junk in Cynder's eyes, which she wasn't interested in. She didn't find any yearbook.

She got the flashlight out of the kitchen drawer and went to the attic. The boxes that her grandmother had used were old and dusty so she tried to stay away from those. She went to the back of the attic and found some boxes that looked like they were in better condition and not quite so dusty. She saw one marked books and pulled it down from the stack.

When she opened the box, a musty smell crept up her

nostrils. At the top of the box she found toddler books that had 'Jessilyn' written on them in crayon. She found old coloring books, a few stuffed toys, and an old plastic doll, that should've been discarded long ago.

At the bottom of the box, she found what she was looking for. There were four of her mother's class yearbooks, but Cynder was most interested in her senior year. She took the book over to the center of the attic so that she could see better beneath the hanging light bulb.

She turned to find the picture of her mother. She looked almost the same, only she wasn't as heavy as she is now and her hair was shorter. She had on a black sweater with a white blouse under it, and she didn't have much of a smile. Below her picture it said that she was in cheerleading for four years. Jessilyn had never mentioned being a cheerleader to Cynder, but then, she never talked about her high school experiences.

She looked up her father's picture and above it someone had written; 'Jessilyn- Jake Tackett will love you forever,' and a little heart was drawn. Cynder smiled warmly at his picture and was sure that Jake had written it. She noticed that she did look a little bit like him. She had his smile. Underneath his picture, it said that he had played basketball and football all four years and was president of his class.

She went to the B's in the book, searching for Eva Black, but when she got there, all she saw was a cutout hole where a picture should have been. Below the hole it said 'Eva Black' and that she was a cheerleader for four years. *My mother must have really hated her in school to do something this serious*, Cynder thought.

Cynder turned to the cheerleading pictures and Eva's face had been scribbled out beyond recognition. Eva stood beside Jessilyn in the picture and she was a lot smaller than her, very petite. Eva's white shoes and socks looked disheveled and old compared to the other cheerleaders. Jessilyn looked happy on the squad of five girls.

She turned to the inside pages of the class book, where people normally wrote salutations at the end of the year. A few girls had signed it, and made brief statements like, have fun with J, take care, and good luck in the future. A few boys wished her good luck.

A girl named Sandy wrote her 'watch your back for you know who.'

One girl wrote, 'Remember when you made that Voodoo doll of EB in art class? I'll look you up if I ever need one, ha ha.' It was signed, Valerie. *Pretty serious,* thought Cynder, *did EB stand for Eva Black and did her mother really try to hurt Eva or was it a joke? Or more importantly, was her mom practicing voodoo?*

One writer wrote, 'I will have JT when you go to college.' It was not signed, but Cynder suspected that Eva wrote this.

At dinner that evening Cynder had so many questions she wanted to ask her mother, about the voodoo, about Eva Black, and about her father. She thought, *I can start on a different topic and then work up to asking about her high school days. I need to be careful how I approach her or she will get mad and leave the room like she usually does.*

"You know that little boy at the school, Grant, that I like so much? Well, Aunt Krystal is having some problems with his mother."

"What did Krystal say?" her mother asked.

"She told me to stay away from her, but also said she is not to go near Grant."

"Then take Krystal's advice," Jessilyn said.

"Oh," Cynder said, in the most innocent voice she could come up with. "Do you know Grant's mother?"

"No," Jessilyn said. She was not interested in the topic at all. Her mother didn't really react much about this news. Maybe this isn't the woman that stole Jake away from her, Cynder thought, or maybe she didn't know that Jake and Eva had a son named Grant that is autistic.

"Well I'm tired; I want to go to bed. Can you clean up the kitchen for me? Thanks." Her mother retired for the evening.

Well that didn't help at all, Cynder thought, *I need to learn how to be a better detective.*

CYNDER

CHAPTER NINETEEN

Tuesday and Wednesday passed with no sightings of Eva. But Cynder was wondering about her. *When children are told to stay away from someone it makes them curious about them,* Cynder thought, *why do people do that to us?* She really wanted to know what went on between Eva and her mother in high school, but Jessilyn was not about to discuss anything with anyone at this time.

Jessilyn wanted to go away to a health spa that could help her with her weight. She had been saving for it for a long time. She explained to Cynder that she wanted to go over the July 4th weekend.

Jessilyn said to Cynder, "I'd like you to stay with Aunt Krystal this weekend."

"Oh, mom," Cynder whined, "I'm old enough to stay alone."

"Not overnight," her mother shook her head, "and this is for three nights."

"I can take care of myself. Besides, Sheridan is going camping with Basha and her family."

"I know you can take care of yourself," her mother agreed, "but it's not you that I don't trust, its other people. How about I get you a cell phone?" Now she was resorting to bribery.

"No cell phone!" All Cynder could picture was Basha texting all of her friends on her cell phone. Cynder didn't have anyone to text.

"We do need to discuss safety procedures sometime. I don't even know where you are half of the time. It seems you keep disappearing on me."

Cynder laughed, "What, mom, you think someone is going to kidnap me?"

"It's not funny Cynder; there are some really evil people out there." Jessilyn changed the subject. "You like Aunt Krystal and Sam; you'll have fun with them."

"Yeah, while they babysit me?"

Jessilyn ignored the comment.

"Krystal wanted you to help her plant some flowers around her yard." Jessilyn said, hoping Cynder would agree to go without a fight.

Cynder did soften up a bit. She figured this would be an opportunity to take the letters from the attic and read them when her mother wasn't around. She was also hoping she could get some information out of her Aunt Krystal about her father and her grandmother.

"I'll make you a deal mom," Cynder said.

"What's that," Jessilyn said reluctantly.

"If you choose to be happy from now on, I will go with them while you're on your spa weekend." Cynder learned that her mother had a choice to be happier than she had been lately.

"I will be happy with a spa weekend," Jessilyn said.

"No," Cynder explained, "You can be happy ALL of the time if you choose to be. So when you get back you will be happy, too. Anyone can choose to be happy if they want to mom. It's a choice anyone can make. What do you say?"

Jessilyn put her right hand up and put her left hand over her chest, "From this day forward I, Jessilyn, choose to be happy." She nodded and gave Cynder a hug.

On Thursday morning Cynder placed the album, the yearbook, the pictures, and letters in her backpack to take them to Krystal's house for the long weekend. She stuffed her clothes and her extra things in the backpack too. As usual she put a water bottle in the side pocket of her bag.

Cynder brought her bike to Sheridan's car and asked him to put it in the trunk. If Aunt Krystal would let her go for a bike ride, she was going out to Jake's. She decided that this was the weekend she was going to tell him that she was his daughter. If her mother finds out that she is visiting him, she may try to put an end to it. So, she wanted to let him know before she lost access to him.

"Why are you bringing your bike?" Sheridan asked.

Cynder walked to the back of his car with it. "I'm getting babysat," she said, "by your parents this weekend and I want my bike. Is that okay with you Mr. Basha?"

"Ha ha ha …" Sheridan retorted. "I wish you could be happy for me and Basha." His cell phone rang.

"Bike," Cynder said pointing to his trunk.

… he placed her bike in the trunk.

At the school everyone was rushing around getting prepared for the three-day 4th of July weekend. Some of the workers, volunteers, and students had left early to start their vacations. Krystal had released all of the office workers and many of the maintenance people and told them to go home early and enjoy their weekend. Ed had left early, stating that he wanted to pick up something special for his wife before he went home.

Cynder took time to go outside to water the new potted plants because it was supposed to be a clear and sunny weekend. The ground plants were watered by an in-ground watering system, but the potted plants would be at risk of drying up. She was watering the plants out front and she noticed the red car, Eva's car, sitting out front. Eva was watching the school again. Instead of bothering Aunt Krystal, Cynder decided to take it upon herself to get rid of her. She put her watering hose down and began to walk towards the car. This was all it took, and Eva fled with her usual reckless-driving escape.

Cynder giggled.

It took Cynder another hour to finish watering all of the potted plants in the back garden. She decided she had better water the inside ones before she left. She was walking past Grant's classroom, so stuck her head in to tell him goodbye for the weekend. The only one in the room was Basha, who was sweeping the floor. Cynder turned to go back out of the room and Eva came rushing in.

Eva looked horrified. "I came in to pick Grant up," she sobbed, "and he ran away from me and went up those cement steps inside the tower. Please help me get him down Cynder, you're the only one that can get him to come to you," she pleaded.

Basha looked up from her sweeping.

Cynder gave Eva a dirty look. She was sure that Eva wasn't supposed to be picking Grant up in the first place. Cynder's arms dropped to her sides. She needed to get Grant away from the tower ballroom.

Eva pulled on Cynder, "Please help me get him," she cried urgently, pulling on her arm, then on her dress.

Cynder had to help Grant. She was going to take him to Aunt Krystal and let her handle the situation.

Cynder picked up her backpack and turned to Basha, "Tell Sheridan I'm going to find Grant and have him leave my bike and I'll ride to Aunt Krystal's later." Cynder reluctantly walked out of the room with Eva. "Which set of steps did he go up?"

CHAPTER TWENTY

Krystal was almost done closing the school up for the long weekend. She rang Sheridan's cell to find out where he was. She went towards Grant's room to lock it up and heard his phone ringing inside the room. When she entered the doorway she saw Sheridan and Basha embraced in a kiss as the phone continued to ring, unanswered, in his pocket.

"Sheridan," Krystal interrupted. Both he and Basha snapped to attention and slightly backed away from each other. "This is very inappropriate," she scolded.

"Mom," Sheridan pleaded, "we are old enough to kiss." His face flushed, never the less.

"I don't disagree with that fact," she explained, "but it is inappropriate to kiss at the school where you are working."

"Oh," they said in unison, both showing their

embarrassment.

"You had better get Basha home and go get your things so you and her family can leave for vacation. I advise you two to cool-it when you're camping."

They both nodded.

Basha grabbed her backpack and headed for the door.

"Sheridan," Krystal said, "I will speak to you about this when you get home from camping." She waved him towards her. "Come here and hug me good bye." She walked over to him and gave him a hug, "And there will be no kissing while you're with her family. Get it?"

He nodded and followed after Basha.

Krystal could hear Basha giggling as they ran down the hall. She shook her head and rolled her eyes, "Young love," she mumbled.

Eva pointed to a set of steps. "He went through the door at the top of those spiral steps in the tower." She pointed to the corner tower just off the lobby. "He kept running from me," she explained to Cynder. She ran up ahead of Cynder on the steps.

Cynder thought this was odd because all of the employees were told that those doors were to remain shut and locked. She didn't trust Eva. Her gut was telling her something was not right about this. Maybe Grant was at the top of the steps, waiting in the dark. He was trying to get away from Eva. He always ran from her.

"Hurry, Cynder." Eva got to the top before Cynder. She poked her head inside the door.

"There he goes again, he ran around to that corner of the room," she pointed into the room. "Please Cynder, will you go get him for me?" she begged. "He'll run away from me again."

Eva stepped back outside into the small landing at the top of the steps.

"Stay here." She instructed Eva to stay outside the room.

"Of course." Eva continued, and pointed towards the door. "He went over to the other side of the room behind that little couch."

Cynder stepped into the dimly lit room. Very little light was coming in through the small glass panes in the windows. She switched the light switch but nothing happened.

"Over there," Eva pointed to the corner furthest from them.

There were a few odd pieces of furniture in the room; one small couch, a few chairs, and some small tables. Cynder walked to the other side of the room and looked behind the furniture. There were no closets or hidden corners in the room. The open ballroom was dismal. It took Cynder less than two minutes to inspect the room to see that Grant was not there.

Cynder walked back towards the door, "He's not…" the door slammed. She ran to it and pushed, but it seemed to be stuck. "He's not in here Ms. Black." She pushed harder on the door with her shoulder, but it wouldn't budge. She heard the deadbolt lock. Eva laughed a sinfully evil laugh. There was no way to unlock it from Cynder's side.

Eva whispered wickedly, "You will never see Grant again. I will have you out of my life forever now, Cynder. Jake will hurt so much when he discovers you have both been taken from him again."

"Let me out Eva," Cynder said with a low growl, while trying to stay calm. She pushed on the door as hard as she could and it wouldn't open. She kicked it and yelled, she was alarmed, but tried not to sound panicky. "Eva, I said to let me out, right now, let me out," she demanded as loudly as she could and shook the door.

Eva is probably already down the steps, she thought.

"Aunt Krystal help me, I'm up in the tower." She yelled and screamed for a few minutes until her throat hurt. "Help me someone!" It was no use; Aunt Krystal was not going to hear her. She began to panic.

She ran to the windows at the front of the building, hoping to get someone's attention. She saw Eva climbing into her red car; she glanced up at Cynder with a nasty grin on her face. Grant was in the back seat pounding on the back window, he saw her. Cynder couldn't hear him but was sure he was screaming "Save me Cinderella, save me!"

Cynder screamed back, "I will save you Grant." Eva

pulled out of the driveway recklessly, tossing Grant around in the backseat of the car. No car seat, no seat belts, nothing to secure him as he bounced around like an empty pop can.

Cynder continued to scream and bang her fists on the small window from the tower. "Grant, I will save you, I will save you." Of course, at the moment Cynder couldn't even save herself.

Her eyes darted to all of the windows in the tower room. She ran around the room checking every one of the narrow windows. There were two on each wall of the rectangular shaped room. None of them were made to open. She checked the other tower door that led to the room and that was locked too.

She peered out the side window near the parking lot. She saw Aunt Krystal's car there. She went back to the door again and yelled and kicked it hard until her legs ached. She heard a car door shut. She ran back to the window and saw Aunt Krystal driving away. She pounded on the window and yelled for her Aunt Krystal as loud as she could, but it was too late, she was gone.

Everyone was gone.

CYNDER

CHAPTER TWENTY ONE

Cynder now wished that she had that cell phone that her mother offered to get her. She started to cry softly. She wondered if her mother had left for the spa yet and might have called Aunt Krystal's house to tell her goodbye. She figured it wouldn't be long before Aunt Krystal would come looking for her. Sheridan would be with Basha right now and she should have told him that she had gone with Eva to look for Grant, so when they couldn't find her they should know where to look.

She decided that crying would not do her any good. She pulled the small couch over by the window and poured her back pack out. She had a bottle of water, some clean clothes, and a photo album, a yearbook, and some letters to read, plus the one picture she had kept in her pocket since she'd found it of her and her grandmother.

She took her clean white dress and cleared the tears from

her eyes and face. She was more worried about Grant than she was for herself.

She decided to read some of the letters as long as she still had light. She told herself that it wouldn't be long before she would be rescued from this place and Jake could go after Eva. She would tell Jake she was his daughter and together they could save Grant.

Jake was in his pottery studio working when he looked up at the clock and saw it was almost five. He usually heard the bus coming and would get out to the road to meet Grant as he got off from the bus. He walked out by the road. Grant should have been dropped off half an hour ago. He wondered if he'd missed hearing the bus because he was working at the pottery wheel.

When he didn't see him in the driveway or near the road, he began to get paranoid. *Had Eva gotten him at the bus stop and driven off with him?* he thought. He ran around the front yard calling for him. He couldn't control his sweat. He swiped his forehead with his hand, leaving a streak of clay across it.

It took him over an hour to check all of the rooms in the house and the buildings and rows of plants on the property. He yelled Grant's name until his throat was raw. Panic began setting in when he realized it would be dark in two hours. His heart raced as he picked up the phone.

Krystal stopped by the grocery store on her way home to get some food for the weekend. She wanted to rent some movies for her and Cynder to watch. She planned to make the weekend special for her. The stores were busy and by the time she got home it was seven o'clock. When she walked in the door she saw a note from her husband, Sam, saying that he was joining the guys for a round of golf and then dinner. He told her he hoped she and Cynder had fun this evening.

"Cynder," she called, as she walked through the house. "I got us some great movies; I hope you haven't seen them yet." She sat down an armful of groceries. "Sam and Sheridan never want to watch these kinds of movies with me, so it'll be a treat for me."

She went back out to the car and got the rest of the bags. She again brought a load and left it on the counter in the kitchen. "Cynder, where are you?"

She looked in the living room and all of the rooms on the first floor and started to go upstairs when her phone rang in the kitchen. She ran to answer it. "Hello."

"This is Jake Tackett, Grant's dad." His voice was shaky and pressured, he sounded extremely upset, and she had never heard him like this.

Jake explained to Krystal that he had checked all over his property, in the buildings, and in the house, but couldn't find Grant.

"Stay there, I'll meet you at your place and help look

again." She hung up the phone and yelled upstairs, "Cynder, Cynder are you there?" There was no answer. She went to the kitchen and threw the cold food into the refrigerator. She left a note for Cynder instructing her to call her on her cell phone when she got there and that she planned a fun movie night for the two of them.

On her way to Jake's house, Krystal called the person in charge of the bus garage. He wasn't home, so she left him a message. Maybe Grant fell asleep on the bus and the driver didn't notice him.

Jessilyn had sat through the introductory session at the spa and was told that they were to shut off all of their cell phones for the weekend to enjoy the total spa experience. She had two hours of free time before dinner. She walked into the spa's beauty salon.

They sat her in a chair. "What would you like done today?" the beautician asked.

"I am choosing to be happy from now on, and I promised this to my daughter," Jessilyn said, "and I think I need to be a completely different person to do that. I want a make-over, a complete make-over. I bought all brightly colored clothes today and I need a new hair color to go with it." She held up both sides of her long, drab, black hair. "First I want all of this mess cut off…chin length I think, any style you want. And what color do you think would look good on me?"

The beautician's eyes lit up. She loved it when a client came in and left it up to their beautician to make these style decisions. She got some beauty magazines out for her and Jessilyn to look through to pick out a whole new look for her.

Sheridan and Basha's family sat at the campfire singing camp songs and roasting hot dogs and marshmallows. Two other families joined their campfire. Every chance Sheridan got, he kissed Basha when no one was looking. Basha's little sister caught them once and giggled. She was playing games on Sheridan's new cell phone, so she was happy.

When Sheridan went to his car to retrieve his sleeping bag and small tent, Basha followed him. Sheridan stole a few kisses while they were in the dark and then told her that they had better get back. "I want your parents to like me. Besides if they told my mom they caught us kissing, I'd be in big trouble."

The sun had gone down completely and they all took turns putting logs on the fire to keep it going. Basha's dad said that after nine o'clock they shouldn't put anymore on, so they could let it die down before they all retired for the night. Sheridan had set up his small tent near the family's big tent.

Cynder read letters until day turned into night in the tower ballroom. She had brought the letters that her grandmother and her mother had written back and forth. She wanted to check the dates on the letters and correlate them so she could see how the conversations went back and forth between her mother and her grandmother.

So far she discovered that her grandmother was happy about Jessilyn's pregnancy. But, the letters were dated before Cynder was born. Grandmother encouraged Jessilyn to stay in Texas and finish her schooling. She promised she would be out to help when the baby was born and she was even thinking about moving out there.

Jessilyn had told her mother about a supportive friend that she went to college with, Krystal, who was married and had a toddler. Krystal was going to help out as much as she could and treated her like family.

This painted a happy picture of life. Cynder wondered when it all went wrong.

Cynder was careful about how much she drank from her only bottle of water. She had no idea how long it would be until someone found her. She scrounged in her backpack for a candy bar or gum or anything to keep her stomach from growling, but found none.

"Shut up, shut up, shut up!" Eva screamed at Grant. She tried swatting at him when she was driving and she almost swerved off the road. "Why can't you ever just sit down and be quiet?" Grant continued to kick and scream in the back seat, pounding himself in the head with his fists.

Eva locked him in the car and went to the nearest pharmacy for some over the counter liquid cold medicine that would help to put him to sleep. She got four bottles of liquid for him and picked up a bottle of sleeping pills for herself and the strongest pain medicine she could get. She had twisted her back badly when she threw Cynder's bike into the bushes at the school.

Cynder…That little horror has always been a thorn in my side, Eva thought, *that's all Jake ever thought about until I gave him a son. His little Cynder, that's all I ever heard, well that and his precious Jessilyn. And now she's come back to my town. If Grant could have behaved when he was a baby I never have would drugged him so heavily. If he could have just sat still and kept quiet, I would have had the perfect life with Jake. He would have eventually gotten all of his family's money and we could be happy. I wouldn't be like my parents, who struggled to put food on the table for seven children. Now Jake's family will pay…* "They will pay."

She stopped by a fast food restaurant and got a milk shake to mix Grant's medicine into. She gave him the shake and a burger and he was quiet for the moment.

Eva figured they would blend in amongst the vacationers if she could get control of Grant. She checked into the Red Roof Inn in Muskegon. She hadn't gone very far, but she could no longer stand Grant's tantrums.

Cynder had settled onto the small couch for the night. She returned the letters to the backpack, they made a nice pillow. She used her extra dress as a blanket and was settling down to sleep. She couldn't figure out why Sheridan or Aunt Krystal had not come for her. Did they even know that Eva had Grant? She planned to contact Grant through a dream to see if she could help him. She had done this several times since the first dream and it seemed to come easily for her. This was the only control she had at this time to save him. She felt exhausted and knew she could fall asleep easily.

She fell off to a deep sleep right away and Grant appeared. She could hear his small voice. "Mommy gave me yucky drugs," he told Cynder. "They taste bad. Mommy is mad at me."

In her dream state Cynder tried to sweep him into her arms to cradle him, but it was like she was a ghost.

She began to make out what was around him. It was as though she was remotely viewing the inside of the motel room. She knew that her body was not really there but her mind was. It was like when she was in the garden at the Landscapes of Eden and she tried to hold the flower bud.

She saw Eva asleep in a bed next to Grant's. He was curled up on top of the bed. Eva hadn't tucked him in or even covered him with a blanket. Cynder tried to pick up the blanket but she couldn't. She tried to shake him awake without success. She saw bottles of liquid cold medicine and pills in the room and fast food bags and cups. The television was on and the blinds were open. She sat in a chair in the room for what felt like hours. She knew she was in a dream, but it felt so much different this time. She wanted to watch over Grant for as long as she could.

In her dream she found herself walking outside of the room like a ghost. She walked right through the door. They were in a motel that had a bright red roof. She saw a sign that said, 'Red Roof Inn of Muskegon.' She turned back to look at the door and saw the number 107, they were on the ground floor.

CYNDER

CHAPTER TWENTY TWO

Krystal and Jake had looked all over his property and up and down the road. They canvassed the neighbors until they had covered two miles each way. Krystal suggested they go to the bus garage. It was pitch black now. They armed themselves with flashlights.

All of the buses were locked. They yelled and beat on the sides of the buses and could not find Grant. Jake boosted Krystal up with his hands in a foothold position but they did not see him on any of the buses.

"I think it's time to call the police," Krystal said, "who could have taken him?"

Jake fell to his knees and began to sob. "Eva…Eva must have taken him. I suspected this right away. That has to be what's going on. I must call my grandfather. I wouldn't put it past her to try blackmailing him or something; she always wanted my family's money."

They were both feeling a lot of guilt at this point.

Krystal knelt beside him. "I didn't see her around the school today. Do you think she got him from the bus?"

"I don't know…I was… I was working in my pottery studio. I didn't hear the bus. They only go by if Grant is on it." He plunged his face into the palms of his hands. "I need to save him from her." He got up from his knees. "I don't have time to feel sorry for myself, I need to find Grant." He wiped his face on his shirt sleeve.

Krystal had trouble not crying herself, but who doesn't when they witness a man sobbing.

Jake called the police.

"Let's drive back to your house. I can make some calls on the way," Krystal told him.

Krystal called the manager of the bus garage, Sheridan, her own home, Jessilyn's home and cell and no one was answering. She was getting frustrated. "I know it's a holiday weekend, but someone needs to pick up their darn phones." She threw her cell phone into her purse.

"Did you get hold of Cynthia?" Jake asked.

"No- no one is answering any phones. She should be at my place but she wasn't when I tried calling there."

"Maybe she's with your husband."

"I doubt that, he went golfing after work and then dinner with his buddies. He won't be home until eleven."

Jake called his grandfather. "Ed, this is Jake. I hate to call you now, I know you and Kalli are having guests this weekend, but I can't find Grant."

He explained to Ed about how Grant did not come home from the bus and how they'd checked the buses. Ed told them he would be right over, the guests had arrived, they've had dinner and now everyone was settling into bed for the night.

"You know us old people," Ed laughed, "We don't stay up late like we used to. I will be right over."

"There's something else Ed…" Jake said.

"What?" Ed asked.

"I think Eva might have him. Has she called your house at all?" Jake inquired. "Have you seen anything of her lately?"

"Only when she was at your house packing up some of her things. As usual she was very cold with me. I know she's been going to the school."

They both paused.

"Have you called the police?" Ed asked. He didn't usually like to use his clout with police, but in a situation like this he would.

"Just now yes, I didn't realize until just now that this might be a crime. They are meeting me at my house."

"See you there." Ed promised.

Cynder drifted in and out of sleep after she remotely saw Grant. She wanted to contact Gilly or Lazuli in her dream state.

She breathed slowly in and out, relaxing as much as she could, and visualized herself walking down the little sidewalk to her garden, the Garden of Lapis. She saw the bright blue fence and looked down to unlatch it.

She noticed she was wearing a blue dress that was the same shade blue as her lapis stone and her hair was clean and shiny and flowing like Lazuli's hair. She knew she was in the dream state. The plants moved, like the ones she imagined when she first walked into the Pleiades school. They were more than alive, they emoted like people and Cynder understand how they felt. The colors of the blooming flowers glowed of colors so brilliant and unearthly colored that Cynder could not assign a single color to one.

Gilly came to her at the entrance to the gate, but to Cynder's surprise she didn't ask Gilly for help to get out of this situation. Instead she asked Gilly, "Why does Lazuli carry a wand and you don't?"

Gilly said, "Not all fairies are allowed to use wands, they are very powerful and can only be in experienced hands. Wands are used to focus magical energy. That means that energy in and around the body gathers in the wand. Then the wand acts like a pointing stick. It can send that magical energy in whatever direction the wand is pointed. Wands help fairies cast magical spells!"

"Magic spells? I don't need magic spells." Cynder said, rejecting any idea of spells.

"Your lapis stone is facilitating this spiritual journey in your dream. You have been gifted a very special stone from the Garden of Lapis, Cynder. Use it carefully in your life."

And then Gilly exploded like a firecracker, a puff of fairy dust blew away in the wind and she was completely gone.

Cynder, still in her dream state, swung the gate open in the Garden of Lapis and saw Sheridan's back as he was sitting on the bench. She expected to see Basha with him, but she was not. She waved to him and he waved back. He had a big smile on his face as he usually does. She walked to the bench and sat next to him. He didn't speak.

She spoke to him, but it wasn't through her mouth. It was like she was thinking it and he understood her. *I need you to rescue Grant.* Sheridan nodded. *Eva has taken him. They are at the Red Roof Inn in Muskegon, room 107. You must go there and get him. Bring him to the Pleiades School.* He nodded.

Sheridan stood up and then she snapped out of the dream and found herself awake in the darkened tower ballroom again.

The police met Jake, Ed, and Krystal at Jake's house. Jake introduced Krystal as the Superintendent of the Pleiades School and Ed as his grandfather. Ed was dressed in fine clothes today. Krystal had seen him dressed like this before, but was surprised again at how different he looked when he cleaned up.

"What makes you think your ex-wife has taken him?" the senior officer asked Jake. He opened a small flip top notebook and was prepared to take notes.

"She lost custody when we divorced. She served time in jail for child abuse so visitation with Grant must be supervised. When she came back and couldn't take him, it made her furious. She had gone away for three years and then she showed up again this summer. She wanted me to give her money and when I wouldn't she said she would make me pay one way or another."

"Do you have a lot of money?" the officer asked, looking up from his notebook.

"I don't have any money myself," Jake motioned to his grandfather, "but my grandfather is Ed Myer."

"Oh," the officer exclaimed and jumped to his feet. "I'm sorry, Mr. Myer, I didn't know that was you." He offered his hand to shake Ed's hand.

Ed shook his hand and motioned for him to sit back down. "Please, I like to keep a low profile."

"Yes, of course said the officer." He thumped the end of his pen on his pad of paper. He looked up at them sympathetically. "I can call an Amber alert out on your son, and put out a warrant for an arrest on Eva."

"Jake," the officer said, "I would like permission to tap both yours and your grandfather's phone lines and I think you should stay around the phone until we hear more. Krystal, you should go get some rest, it's almost midnight."

CYNDER

CHAPTER TWENTY THREE

Krystal drove to her house and found Sam asleep with all of the lights on in the house. He jumped up when she touched his hand.

"I've been trying to get hold of you for two hours now," he said, "where have you been?"

"Oh," she pulled out her cell phone and noticed it had gone dead. "Sam, I am so sorry. I had tried the house many times and made so many calls today; I didn't notice it was dead."

She explained about Grant being missing and the search for him.

"I'm glad you're finally home safe. I'm sorry about Grant, we will find him together. Does Cynder know?"

"If you didn't tell her, then I guess she doesn't know."

"What do you mean...she isn't here," Sam revealed. "I saw the note you left her and figured you two had gone out."

"No...no...no, I don't understand what's going on." Krystal shook her head, put her hands to the sides of her cheeks, and collapsed on the sofa.

Sam got the phone to call the police.

Jessilyn was up early in the morning for a healthy breakfast, yoga, and walking on the beach at the spa. She knew that all of this was supposed to be relaxing; she had saved for it for years and was looking forward to it. This was the first time she had left Cynder for any length of time. She told another woman at the spa, "I feel so guilty about leaving."

"It's just because you are used to helping and doing for others instead of thinking of yourself," she told Jessilyn.

"No, that's not it," Jessilyn said, "I feel that something awful is going on back home. I really would like to call my best friend and make sure everything is alright."

"We all made a promise not to use our cell phones. Have lunch with me first," the woman said, "and then we have booked massages. If you're still feeling tense about things after that, you can call."

"Okay," Jessilyn promised. "But, I wish I could call now." She forced a smile. She hesitated as they walked to the patio for lunch. She forced herself to sit for lunch but her stomach was wound up. She found herself with no appetite.

Krystal and Sam got up that morning and headed for Jake's to meet with the police. No one had heard from Eva or Cynder. Ed pulled in right behind them in his big black Cadillac. Ed had left his wife, Kalli, home with an officer to man the phones.

After Krystal revealed to the police that Cynthia was a teenager that had problems with her mother, the case took on a new twist. The police were convinced that she had done something to Grant.

It took nearly two hours for Krystal, Jake, and Ed to convince the police that Cynthia would do nothing to harm Grant.

The police asked Krystal to continue to contact the bus employees and Jessilyn. She also tried to call Sheridan without any luck.

Cynder woke to bright rays of light that bounced off the dust that hung in the tower ballroom. She vaguely remembered her dreams and hoped that she got through to Sheridan.

The day was bright and sunny as the weatherman had

promised. She peered at the colors of the flowers in the back garden and admired how well they had come together. She saw hummingbirds and butterflies enjoying them also

She looked at her fists and they were black and blue from banging on the doors and windows yesterday. She felt defeated and was losing all hope. It upset her when she thought about how far away Eva had gotten with Grant. Surely Jake and the police would be looking for her.

She went from window to window throughout the morning hoping that someone would see her or come looking for her.

By the time Sheridan rolled out of his sleeping bag it was almost nine o'clock and Basha's mother was frying bacon over the fire. Basha ran to him and threw her arms around him. Sheridan felt a little embarrassed and pushed her back gently.

"Did you sleep well?" Basha asked.

Sheridan rubbed his forehead. "Yeah, but I had the weirdest dream. Something about Cynder and a red roof. I don't know." He shrugged his shoulders. Basha frowned at the mention of his dreaming about Cynder.

"Who is Cynder?" Basha's mother asked.

Basha jumped right in with an explanation, "She's this little girl that tags along after Sheridan. I'm surprised he got away from her this weekend."

Her mother looked at Sheridan. "Really," he said, "she's like my little cousin. Our mother's have known each other since we were young. She calls my mother Aunt and I the same with her mother. We are very close, that's all."

"It sounds nice," her mother said.

"At the school Cynder dotes on this little autistic boy named Grant," Basha said. She was jealous of Cynder with Grant too.

"Grant-" Sheridan said loudly, snapping his fingers. "I am supposed to help Grant," he spoke very quickly. "Cynder needs me to get Grant. I need to go help." Sheridan ran back to his tent and tore it down. He grabbed the end of his sleeping bag and dragged both of them to his car and tossed them into the trunk.

Basha followed him begging for an explanation.

He stepped back over to her mother and made apologies that he had to go. Basha's little sister held his cell phone out to him. He thanked her and threw it into his pocket.

"I don't understand," Basha cried, "all because of a dream. This is crazy Sheridan, you can't go." She put her arms around him and tried to hold him back.

"I need to go Basha. They need me."

"I need you," Basha begged.

Sheridan pushed her arms down to her sides. "I will text you later, I'm sorry." He nodded to the rest of the family and got into his car.

After lunch Jessilyn went to the massage room. She lay on the massage table and tried to prepare for the session. She felt uneasy and she couldn't figure out why. She thought it might be because she hadn't let anyone massage her since she was in massage school.

"Just relax," the woman told her. "Is this music alright?"

"Yes," Jessilyn responded. She took several deep measured breaths and tried to relax. She could not get Cynder off from her mind. She felt like Cynder needed her right now. Jessilyn knew that she shouldn't feel guilty that she left her for the weekend, but she had an overwhelming feeling of dread.

After ten minutes of trying to relax, she said, "I'm sorry, I can't relax. It's not you, it's just…for some reason I feel like I'm needed at home. I can't do this. I will still pay, but I must go."

She scrambled to her room and got her things and off she went.

Krystal and Jake were out of answers for the police. They had thoroughly checked Jake's property and the buses again. The police had canvassed the neighborhood and the town.

Krystal continued, frantically, to call the manager of the bus garage, Jessilyn, and Sheridan. She wished she would have gotten Basha's number and her mother's number, but it was too late now. She didn't know which campground they had gone to and she didn't ask Jessilyn which spa she visited. Krystal was used to covering all of the safety rules concerning school business, but when it came to her own family she fell short.

"Don't be so hard on yourself," Sam pleaded. "I didn't ask those questions either, and it shouldn't always be left up to you." He wrapped his arms around her and kissed the top of her head.

"I'm sure Eva did something to both of them," Jake said, "She is cunning and manipulative, and a bit on the-" he looked around, "well, crazy side."

The Chief of Police explained that they had contacted the State Police. "They will ask all of you the same questions and more. I haven't decided if we should put out an Amber Alert for Cynthia or consider her a suspect-"

Krystal got after him when he said this. "I can assure you she would not do anything to put Grant at risk. I have known this girl since she was little and you are out of line suspecting her."

He backed off and decided to let the State Police deal with Krystal and the situation.

CYNDER

CHAPTER TWENTY FOUR

Sheridan pulled slowly into the Red Roof Inn. He thought he remembered the room as 107. He parked down on the end of building far away from the door of 107.

He walked casually past the room and could see Grant sitting on the edge of the bed. Eva was sleeping. He turned around, went back to their room, and stood by the window peering in with just his face. He brought his hand up slowly near his face and waved in slow motion until Grant looked up. He could see that Grant recognized him. Grant looked at the empty chair in the room for a few minutes as though he saw something there, but it was difficult to tell what went on behind the eyes of an autistic child. Sheridan continued to wave slowly. Grant looked back at Eva and then back at Sheridan.

Sheridan laid his pointer finger across his lips to signal for Grant to be quiet. Grant mimicked his movement. Sheridan pointed towards the door and motioned Grant to go to it. Grant glanced back at Eva again then back at Sheridan. He slipped off from the bed and slowly headed toward the door. He stopped at the empty chair and put his hand on the seat. Sheridan waved a little faster and motioned toward the door again.

Eva began squirming around and rolled over to her back. She started to snore loudly. She startled Grant and he jerked his head to look at her.

Sheridan got on his knees and crawled near the door.

Grant walked to the door and turned the knob a little and Sheridan opened the door slightly, and gently took Grant's hand and eased him out of the room.

Sheridan was still on his knees. "Hello Grant," he whispered. This was the first time Grant had ever let Sheridan touch him.

Sheridan and Grant walked slowly to Sheridan's car. Sheridan opened the door and Grant climbed into the shot-gun seat. "No," Sheridan whispered, "Back here."

Grant would not move. "Save Cinderella, save Cinderella," he said getting louder and louder. Sheridan buckled him in and ran to the other side of the car. He idled out of the parking lot and onto the highway.

Jessilyn had gone down the road a few miles when she

remembered that her cell phone was in her suitcase. She decided she would look for it the next time she stopped.

She felt better knowing that she was going home to Cynder. She tried to picture what she would be doing right now. Probably working with Krystal out in the yard telling her about all of the gardening rules that she was breaking.

Before she pulled onto US 31 she decided to pull over and get out her phone. She turned it on and set it on the seat. She took off and was pulling onto the highway when it beeped saying that she had a message.

She wasn't used to viewing her cell phone while she drove so she left it there for the moment until she needed to stop for gas.

Sheridan was making good time on his way home. He wanted to call his mother on his cell phone. It was in his pocket and he was swerving all over the road trying to get it out. His car began to clank and surge. He looked down at the dash. It had stalled and all of the dash lights were lighting up. He had run out of gas.

"Save Cinderella, save Cinderella," Grant protested when the car came to a sudden stop.

Sheridan stood outside of the car and pulled his cell phone out of his pocket. The battery was dead. He realized that he forgot to bring the charger with him. He knew that he would be grounded when he got home. He was irresponsible.

He ran out of gas and now the new cell phone that his mother had gotten him for emergencies could not be used because he let Basha's sister run the battery out and he forgot the charger. He would be in so much trouble when he got home.

Jessilyn saw a car stopped by the side of the road. The boy looked familiar. "Oh my goodness, that's Sheridan," she said to herself.

She pulled in behind him.

By now Grant was having a full fit in the car banging his head over and over again on the seat, yelling about Cinderella. Sheridan didn't know what to do. He saw the car pull over. He hopped it wasn't Eva following him.

He saw that it was Jessilyn. "Aunt Jessilyn," he screamed, "help me."

She picked up her phone and was listening to the message while she walked towards Sheridan. "Oh my goodness," she shouted to him. "Grant is missing, we need to go." She flipped her phone shut.

"I barely recognized you." He pointed to his car. "I know he was missing, but I have him now."

When she got close to the car she heard and saw Grant having a fit. "Is this Grant? Sheridan, why do you have him, your mom says that he is missing."

"It's a long story. Please help me get Grant into your car and then we can take him home. Once we get him to be quiet, can I use your phone to call my mom?"

"Yes, of course, but you have a lot of explaining to do," Jessilyn told him.

Eva had finally slept off her sleeping pills a little after ten o'clock. She woke to find Grant's bed empty. She called to him and looked under both beds. She went into the bathroom looking for him. "You little brat, where are..."

When she didn't see him in the bathroom, she whipped around and saw that the door to the room was not shut tight. She was confused. She didn't know if he'd escaped or if someone had taken him out. *Did Jake find us? Did he report me to the police? Is Grant wandering around outside in the parking lot?*

She gathered up her things. Took the last two bottles of liquid cold medicine and threw them into her purse. She debated whether to look for Grant or make a run for it. When she left her room she was making sure not to look panicked because she didn't want to draw attention to herself.

Grant had calmed down when Jessilyn asked him if he wanted to ride in Cinderella's mommy's car to go see her. He even let her put him in the back seat to buckle him in. She had Sheridan explain everything to her before she would let him use her phone.

"Cinderella, save Cinderella, in my castle," Grant continued to repeat, while Sheridan explained a rather strange dream to Jessilyn and how he rescued Grant.

Sheridan tried again and again to get Krystal by the home phone and her cell phone, but he kept getting the answering system.

The closer they got to Grand Aster, the louder and more excited Grant became.

"Is he always like this?" Jessilyn asked.

"Never," Sheridan said. "He's usually so quiet. The only one that can get him to speak is Cynder."

Jessilyn looked impressed and proud.

"I don't know what would happen if he wasn't buckled," Sheridan confessed, "I have a lot to learn in working with Autistic students."

"Cinderella on top of my castle," Grant chanted, "Save her."

Krystal's phone rang, "This is Ms. Sue, Grant's bus driver."

"Yes," Krystal said, "we've been waiting to hear from

you. When you dropped Grant off yesterday, where did he go?"

"Grant didn't ride the bus yesterday."

"What?" Krystal turned and whispered this message to the people in the room.

Everyone in the room became silent as she continued on with her call.

Ms. Sue said, "He was in line with the rest of the kids, like he usually is, and then all of a sudden he shot off runnin' in the school yard. Some woman with short dark hair waved to me and said she was his momma and she was there to get him. She took off after him." Ms. Sue stopped talking for a moment, when Krystal didn't respond, she asked, "Am I in trouble Ms. Krystal?"

Cynder was losing hope. Her water was almost gone. She was starving and dusty and all she could think of, besides saving Grant, was getting home to her mother. She didn't think she would miss her at all this weekend, but now, she really needed her.

She read more letters to take her mind off from her situation. She discovered that her grandmother had welcomed her with open arms until Cynder's second birthday when she found out that Jake was her father. Grandmother vowed to disown Jessilyn and she kept her word, right up to the day she died. It was true, as Jake had told her, that grandmother was bitter over losing her boyfriend in high school and was making everybody pay dearly for it. She was not happy with Jessilyn's father, and he left her long ago and died a young man. This, she even blamed on Jake's mother. She had so much hatred for Jake's mother; she couldn't stand the thought of having Jake with Jessilyn.

Cynder cried and cried some more. Then she took the treasured photo of her and her grandmother out of her pocket and put it on the last page of the photo album. She couldn't believe that a person could have that much hate in their heart.

"I choose to be happy," she said out loud to herself.

Then she heard Lazuli speak, "I knew you would, my child."

Cynder looked all over and up and down and she didn't see her at all. No Lazuli, no lapis wand, and no magic door.

CHAPTER TWENTY FIVE

"I have a missed call from Jess," Krystal shrieked. "I need to call her back." The chatter in the room stopped and she put the call through.

"Hello," Sheridan answered on Jessilyn's phone.

Krystal jerked her head back in surprise. Everyone in the room became concerned. She finally recognized his voice. "Sheridan? I thought I dialed Jessilyn's number." She pulled the phone away from her ear and looked at the readout.

"Mom… mom? Mom, this is Jessilyn's phone. I am with her and so is Grant."

"How, what, when did…oh never mind all of that." She

announced to the room that Grant was with Sheridan. The chatter rose to a greater level. "Is Cynthia with you too?" Krystal asked hopefully.

"No." Sheridan threw Jessilyn a look of confusion.

"What?" Jessilyn whispered.

"Isn't Cynder supposed to be with my mom?" Sheridan asked Jessilyn.

"Of course." Jessilyn paused, "Isn't she?" This confirmed what she had been feeling.

Sheridan addressed his mother again. "Mom where is Cynder?"

"I don't know, and if you don't know, and Jess doesn't know…" Krystal started crying and handed the phone to Sam. "Cynthia is not with them."

The room was filled with mixed emotions and questions from every-which-way.

Sam and Sheridan calmly discussed how Grant came to be with them. Sheridan told his father of the strange dream and the escape from Eva. He decided to save the part about running out of gas and his cell phone until latter.

Sam stepped outside to talk to Sheridan. "You need to get the boy home, right now, to his father. Keep Jessilyn calm, but let her know that we can't find Cynthia."

Jessilyn went to turn off onto Krystal's road. Grant became very angry and kicked and screamed and banged his head on the seat. "Cinderella in castle, I will save Cinderella."

Jessilyn brought the car to a screeching halt. "Where is the castle Grant? Where is the castle that Cinderella is in?"

"With the stars, castle with the stars," Grant whispered.

"Where is a castle with stars?" Jessilyn asked Sheridan.

"The Pleiades? Grant, at the school, the castle at the school?" Sheridan asked.

Grant nodded his head yes. Jessilyn turned the car in the direction of the school and Grant calmed down.

Jessilyn handed Sheridan her cell phone. "Tell them to meet us at the school. I'm going to help Grant save our Cinderella."

They all pulled into the drive of the school at the same time; Jessilyn with Sheridan and Grant, Sam with Krystal, and the police car with two officers. Drawing up the rear of the parade was Ed and Jake in Ed's shiny black Cadillac.

Cynder didn't see them coming. She had been silently trying to summon Lazuli or Gilly, and then she tried to get through to Grant and Sheridan. She fell into a deep sleep from exhaustion and lack of food and water.

They all piled out of their cars at once.

Jake ran towards Grant, who was the first one out of the car. "Cinderella I will save you." He ran toward the school.

A police officer dragged Cynder's bicycle from the bushes.

"That's hers," Sheridan yelled. "Grant's right, she's here."

The police followed Krystal towards the front door.

Ed stopped and picked up something in the middle of the circle drive by the water fountain. He called Krystal back. "Doesn't this belong to Cynthia?" He held in his hand the small fairy statue, which was in Cynder's likeness, and she had given to Grant.

"Yes, it is hers, I gave it to her when she was little," Krystal said.

Grant ran back and took the statue from Ed.

"She gave it to Grant yesterday," Sheridan said. "Grant must have dropped it when Eva kidnapped him."

No one had noticed the red car at the edge of the side parking lot when they pulled in. Now it was speeding up and aimed right towards Jake. Grant screamed, "Evil coming, evil coming," and he pointed towards the car. Jake and everyone else turned to see what he was yelling about.

Eva's car was picking up speed and headed towards Jake. He ran towards the building and attempted to duck around one of the tower structures to avoid getting run over by Eva. Her car charged onto the ramp, became airborne, and flew over the moat. It was headed right for Jake.

Eva crashed her car full blast into the tower and the front of the car buried itself in the round tower and stopped instantly.

The entire tower collapsed in a heap on top of Eva's car. The brick pile buried most of the car.

For a moment, everything was chaos.

A cloud of dust shot out from the rubble. Jake ran out from it coughing and covered in dust, but he was unharmed.

The impact of Eva's car jolted Cynder from her sleep and threw her onto the floor. Her backpack, spinning like a top, sprayed the photos across the ballroom floor. Cynder watched as they got swept up in a cloud of dust that consumed the air in the ballroom. Cynder tried to get to her feet and was knocked down over and over again as the corner tower crumbled from the building; she backed up again and again to keep from being swallowed by the collapsing ballroom floor. She could barely breathe and pulled her dress up to her face to filter the dust from the air. She could only manage shallow breaths.

Grant was down below jumping up and down, flapping his arms and screaming, "Cinderella, I will save you." Jake had to grab him to keep him from running towards the falling bricks.

Jessilyn ran over to the rubble and screamed, "Cynder."

Jake heard the name, 'Cynder' and spun around on his heels. "Cynder?" he questioned loudly, trying to see who in the crowd had yelled this name.

Cynder finally got her bearings and carefully crawled to the edge of the open floor where the outside wall had collapsed. It continued to crumble, and bricks tumbled out like loose teeth.

Her appearance was frightening. Her hair was a mess, her white dress was dusty, and now the debris from the bricks and rubble had coated her with a tan dust. Dust clung to her clothes, to her hair, to her skin, even to her teeth. She coughed and spat like Ed's old truck.

Cynder heard Jessilyn yelling. She thought she spotted her down on the lawn in a bright red outfit. "Mom is that you?" Instead of being concerned about her own safety, she yelled, "What happened to your hair, its red?" Then Cynder looked into the yard and saw the crowd below. She waved to everyone like she was a celebrity, "Grant, Jake, Sheridan, Ed…" she went through the whole group by name.

She didn't realize she was still in danger. The bricks were crumbling beneath her.

"Cynder get back away from the edge," Jessilyn shouted.

Jake ran around in front of Jessilyn to face her.

"Jessilyn, what are you doing here?" He looked up at

Cynder. "Is Cynthia our little Cynder?"

Jessilyn started to answer him when out of the cloud of dust hanging in the air at ground level; she heard a deep guttural screech that sounded like a hawk going for its prey.

"EEEEeeekkk," Eva screamed, "I hate Cynder, that little brat ruined my life!" She charged toward Jake with her nails out, ready to attack, but before she got to him Jessilyn took a leap and intercepted her, tackling her to the ground. Her small body was a mass of dust and blood, barely looking human.

Jessilyn looked like a trained cop when she flipped Eva over and positioned her arms to be cuffed. She bent over and spoke in Eva's ear. "If you harmed one single hair on our little Cynder's head, you will be sorry," she vowed in a low deep voice.

"Mom, mom, I'm okay, I'm alright. Just get me out of here," Cynder bellowed.

As the police cuffed Eva the whole crowd clapped and cheered. Cynder heard fireworks exploding over the garden and was sure that Gilly must have been watching all of the action. It was like the grand finale that comes at the end of a great fireworks show. Everyone else thought it was just a local show, but Cynder knew it was Gilly showing off.

CYNDER

CHAPTER TWENTY SIX

Once Eva was secured by the police, everyone rushed inside the school to save Cynder. They had to knock the ballroom door down with an ax because the keys were gone from the office. They figured only Eva knew where they were and she wasn't talking. Jake manned the ax and had it knocked down in no time.

Cynder rushed to her mother's arms. "Mom, I missed you so much." They held each other tight. "Great take down on that witch."

Jessilyn pulled back from her, "Careful with the mouth," she warned. They both laughed. "But for once I agree with you."

"I love your new hair and your red outfit looks great on you," Cynder said. "When this is over, will you take me shopping?"

"Anytime, but first we need to get a cell phone for you- in case of an emergency, like a kidnapping or something." They laughed and hugged again.

Jessilyn left the ballroom and headed down the steps. Cynder started to follow her when Jake grabbed her by the arm and pulled her back to him. He said, "Cynder, give your father a hug." For once, Cynder did as she was told. He hugged her tight and gave her a kiss on the top of her head. They both cried happy tears.

Grant attached himself to Cynder too. "You save me and then I save you," he said.

"You were so right Grant, I'm sorry I ever doubted you."

Jake said, "We need to get out of here before this whole floor gives way."

Once they all got out of the ballroom Cynder asked her mother, "What do you think of Jake?" She glanced over in his direction. Then she looked back to Jessilyn, "I know he's my father."

"What?" Jessilyn's mouth fell open and her face turned red. "We have a lot to talk about little Ms. Cynder."

"So do you and Jake," Cynder said, smiling over her shoulder as she walked away.

She swept Grant up in her arms and danced a celebration with him.

It was difficult to name one hero from this incident. For once, there seemed to be more heroes than victims and when the news reporters came out to take pictures and try to write down the order in which things progressed that day, they gave up for the moment and joined the party that was taking place inside the school cafeteria.

"Ed," Cynder said, "why are you all dressed up? I hardly recognized you."

"Well he only owns the Pleiades and half the town," the Grand Aster Chief of Police revealed.

Cynder said, "Really Ed?"

He nodded yes to Cynder.

News people surrounded him when they heard that. They stuck microphones in his face. They questioned him about the kidnapping of his great-grandson. "How much did she ask for ransom?" and "Did that woman have a grudge against you?" and "Who is she, where did she come from?" "Is she crazy?"

None of their questions indicated that they had any idea what had happened. Ed, like everyone else, was still trying to figure it out. He declined an interview and had the police escort all of them off from the property so they could celebrate the safe recovery of Grant and Cynthia.

Ms. Kalli was at Ed's side. Cynder had no idea that the tour guide was Ed's wife. Ms. Sue, the bus driver was called in to celebrate with them too.

Sheridan and Cynder played with Grant and some of the

other students. Grant was handling the crowd better than Krystal expected him too. She remarked to Sam about how much better he had been since knowing Cynder.

"Sheridan," Cynder said, "When did Basha tell you about Eva tricking me?"

"What are you talking about?" Sheridan asked with a puzzled look on his face.

"I asked her to tell you that I went to help Eva find Grant."

His face was blank. He shook his head back and forth slowly.

"When I asked her to have you leave my bike?" Cynder nodded her head yes.

Sheridan shook his head no. "She didn't tell me anything Cynder, I'm sorry." Sheridan said, "I think I need to call her..." he reached for his phone in his pocket, and then stopped. "Tomorrow," he added. He and Cynder smiled at each other. "It was Grant who led us to you." He told her about the dream and how it helped him rescue Grant and how Jessilyn helped them when he ran out of gas. He said, "Grant kept repeating, make that demanding, that we needed to save Cinderella at the castle. I had never heard him talk so much. Your mom finally got him to calm down and he let us know you were here."

"My little brother," Cynder said, leaving Sheridan more confused than ever. And just then it occurred to Cynder that Ed must be her great-grandfather. *That's good,* she thought to herself, *because I already know him so well and I like him.*

Cynder looked over at her mother and Jake. They couldn't take their eyes off from each other. Jake had a silly grin and was talking non-stop. Her mother had a beaming expression on her face and her cheeks glowed. Cynder had never seen her look so happy or so beautiful. And without Jessilyn's dismal baggy dress and the witchy long black hair, she really didn't look heavy anymore.

"Look at mom and Jake," Cynder said to Sheridan, "do you think they are in love?"

Sheridan shrugged his shoulders.

"Jessilyn, you look absolutely radiant," Jake said, "and Cynder is beautiful as well. You have done such a good job." He wanted to put his arms around her, but resisted. "I knew she was special and now I know why." They both glanced at Cynder, who was avoiding both of them for the time being. "Did she tell you how much time she spent with me?"

Jessilyn's jaw dropped. "She told you she was your daughter?"

Jake shook his head. "No, never, didn't have a clue."

"And you never suspected?"

"No, never, didn't have a clue."

"So you didn't know I was in town?" Jessilyn said, flirtatiously.

"No, never, didn't have a clue," he repeated.

Jessilyn slugged him in the shoulder.

Jake laughed, "It feels like high school again," he smiled at her. "Doesn't it?" he asked timidly, while he gently slipped his arm around her.

THE END

(But, see the remaining pages for bonus materials)

C. Logan Anthony

ABOUT THE AUTHOR

Cynthia Logan Anthony, PhD is married and lives in Michigan. She has four children and eight grandchildren, all of whom influence her life and her writings. She is a Psychologist, author, and speaker. She has earned her Doctor of Philosophy in Naturology. She has a private psychology practice and uses holistic healing methods to help children and adults deal with emotional issues. Hypnosis is her favorite therapy besides talk therapy. She currently writes for Healthy & Fit Magazine, distributed out of Lansing, Michigan.

She has been a college instructor and has worked in public schools, teaching and counseling. She has worked as a psychologist in many settings, including private practices, jails, and prisons.

She gets her inspiration for story ideas from, dreams, an active imagination, writer's groups, reading, and real life experiences. She runs a writer's group for women and loves to coach others to meet their writing goals.

A NOTE FROM THE AUTHOR

Cynder in the Garden of Lapis was a story that resulted from a writer's group exercise. I took it further to include the fairy statues that my friend had been giving me for years. This same friend's son was the influence for Cynder helping an autistic boy in the novel. I never knew how the fairies would fit into my life until my character, Cynder, needed a friend. I included the healing Lapis Stone and the Dream Work because of my love for Holistic Health and Alternative Healing Methods. I do believe that our dreams provide us with guidance, ideas, and the ability to heal ourselves. I use Dream Work to assist me in my writing and other areas of my life. I had always been told that I should be a writer and it took me years to finally get started on it. I encourage others not to wait so long.

BONUS MATERIALS

Book Clubs

Processing Questions about the story for Young Adult, Adult, Teachers, or Counseling Groups. These can help Readers understand a little bit more about their own emotions.

1. Do you ever have trouble talking to one of your parents? If yes, what makes it difficult?

2. Do you ever have feelings that you just can't understand?

3. Cynder is going through a transition in her life; turning fourteen, starting high school, and expectations from others. Do you go through any of the emotional ups and downs that Cynder goes through in this story?

4. Cynder finds herself lost in her world. She feels she is nothing like her mother and without knowing her father or other relatives, she is having trouble identifying with anyone. Who do you identify with? If you have no one, who do you look up to?

5. Have you ever thought of taking your own life like Cynder was thinking? If yes, how serious were you and did you tell anyone?

6. If you had a friend that let you know that they wanted to take their own life, would you tell anyone? If yes, who would you tell? If no, why wouldn't you tell?

7. Cynder suddenly looked at her world differently when the fairies told her of her special gift. Did anything in your life ever trigger you to take a different look at your life? Would you ever consider volunteering to work with autistic children?

8. Cynder was able to be a positive influence for her mother. Did you or anyone you know have this kind of relationship with an adult?

9. Jessilyn got defensive when Cynder tried to talk to her about her life and did anything to avoid talking to Cynder about it. Do you or anyone that you know have to deal with a person that had trouble communicating like this?

10. If you had a child like Cynder how would you try to help her grow up?

11. Jessilyn was oblivious to Cynder's feelings. Did you have a parent that was like this with you? How did you handle it?

12. Cynder was jealous of Basha and she couldn't understand why. Have you ever felt like this?

13. Cynder learned that everyone can choose to be happy in life. Do you believe it is possible to make this choice? Why or why not?

14. Have you ever wished that you had some mystical powers? What would they be and how would you use them?

15. Cynder and Jessilyn are stubborn people. Do you think that they learned this from each other, or do you think people are born this way?

Bonus for young writers

Assignments for Teachers, Home Schooling Parents, or Writers to use for story creation:

Write a short story between 1,000 and 4,000 words using the following prompts (you may use all of them or only a few):

1. Choose an object, similar to Cynder's statue; it could be a toy or stuffed animal, a picture, or an

avatar. Give this object special power. Make up a story in which you or some other character becomes friends with this character that you made up from the object.

2. Give these characters positive and negative traits.
3. What troubles do they have in the story? What conflicts do the characters have?
4. What kind of problem could they solve? Maybe it is one that you or someone you know has had to deal with.
5. The solution of the problem will cause changes in your main character. What are those changes.
6. Write a surprise ending that is unusual and unexpected.

(Story Help)

You can cut out pictures from a magazine or get them from the internet. Use a person, famous or not, an animal and a scene that you like. Start making up a story that goes on between the pictures.

Make up conversations that they might have with you or each other. Pretend you take these characters with you to the mall, out to eat, or to school. How would they act and what would they say to you? Talk about clothes, food, other people, or problems you have. Do this for a week and then try to make up a story about them.

CYNDER

C. Logan Anthony